IRO

IRO
SHADES OF LOVE

A Collection of Short Stories by
Rahul Subramanian

To the people
who have added
to the palette of my life

CONTENTS

ACKNOWLEDGEMENTS

I would like to begin by thanking my publisher Bharath Parthasarathy for believing in me and for giving me a chance. The team at 16Leaves has brought this book to fruition and made the process an enriching journey.

I'd also like to thank my family and friends for giving me constant support and encouragement to ultimately reach this point.

IRO

I was always alone. Not exactly alone. I always had crayons beside me when I was a child. I also had a name which I rarely thought about. As I grew up, the crayons turned into paint. The paper turned into a full-size canvas. As I ventured out into the city, all I could see was a grey hue to everything. The entire city looked drab and lifeless. When I stared into the mirror, I saw my white dress splattered with bright colours. I was the only one who could identify each colour. I wasn't visible to anyone else. I was living in my own world. The thought never affected me much. I just kept painting and painting, trying out new styles, climbing tall buildings and looking at the scenery, free to fill in my own colours. This grey world turned into something magical on my canvas. Before I knew it, I was already a grown woman. Something changed. I started to get less excited about painting. I ran out of inspiration. I struggled to pick up the brush. As I looked around my room and saw my paintings scattered everywhere, I ceased to feel the magic. The colours looked lifeless.

"Maybe this is called loneliness."

I guess all this time, I wanted someone to enjoy this world with me. But, the world outside is different. This room is my world. There can never be a harmonious blend. After a few days, I was unable to lift the paintbrush at all. My mind was shut off completely. I aimlessly wandered across the streets. I sometimes knelt down in the middle of the street, unable to move further. Warm tears flowed down my face.

"I don't want to feel like this."

As life continued moving around me, I sat down in the middle of that grey world, slowly losing my own colour. Suddenly, a man knelt down next to me. He placed a hand on my shoulder.

"Are you ok?"

I looked at him surprised.

"How did you notice me?"

He nodded.

"You're quite hard to ignore. You feel like you're from a different world."

He touched my hair.

"These colours look so pretty."

He then quickly stepped away.

"Oh, I'm sorry. I overstepped my bounds. May I ask why you're crying?"

I wiped my tears.

"It's ok," I reassured him. "I didn't expect anyone to be able to notice me."

He looked at me concerned.

"You don't have to worry. You can just carry on."

I turned back but before I could walk away, I felt him grab my hand.

"I can't simply go back. This new world you've shown me, it's too beautiful to ignore."

My mind went blank. Wasn't this what I used to think as well? No. This can't be happening. I've been alone for so many years now. This is not real.

"Can you let go of my hand?"

The moment he let go, I took a few steps forward.

"Don't get involved with me."

"But I …" he was hesitant.

I turned and looked at him pleadingly.

"Don't, please just go away."

I walked back slowly, taking care not to look back at him. I reached and closed the door. Walking to my room I sat down with my head between my knees. What is happening? A person could actually see me. He was able to enter my world. Why did I push him away? What am I scared of? As I kept pondering on these questions, I never realized that the colours in my room had brightened up slightly.

After a few days, I again decided to get some fresh air and walked out of my house. And lo! Sitting across the road in front of my house, leaning on the telephone pole, was that same man. He had changed quite a lot, I noticed. While his entire body was completely grey before, now, I could see him in his colours. Messy black hair, dark black eyes, fair skin covered with a bright white shirt and a black tie. He looked alluring. He looked at me and got up earnestly.

"I know you told me to leave you alone, but I can't do it."

I stayed silent while he kept on talking.

"I want to know more about you. I want to know more about these colours. I noticed myself changing. I got more excited and curious. I want to see more colours. I want to experience more. I want to see the world through your eyes."

I smiled and looked up at him.

"Lumine."

He looked at me confused.

"It's my name. Lumine."

I held my hand out to him.

"I'm Grisha."

He shook my hand softly.

I looked at Grisha and noticed with a smile that he kept staring at me.

"Is there something on my face?"

"No. It's just that your hair looks beautiful. May I touch it?"

"Go ahead", I smiled wider.

Before he could touch my hair, I could distinctly hear his stomach growling loudly.

I laughed while he looked away, fiercely blushing.

"Maybe later. Why don't you come inside?"

I invited him in.

I cooked him a quick meal while he looked around inside my house. After eating, he stood staring at the walls. He then gestured at me frantically with inquisitive eyes.

"What colour is this?"

He repeated the same question several times as his eyes scanned the paintings in the house. Each time, his eyes glowed with excitement. It felt as if I just brought home a new dog. I finally led him to my studio. As I opened the door, he let out a big gasp. He looked around the room ecstatically. We spent the entire night watching the paintings and talking a lot about all my different paintings. I broke away from the conversation to get myself a cup of coffee. When I came back, I saw Grisha sitting in the corner, deep in sleep with his head against the wall. I chuckled and grabbed a blanket from my bedroom. I covered him and made him somewhat comfortable taking care not to wake him and sat in front of him.

"What is he so happy about?"

I smiled as Grisha slept peacefully. Grisha used to stay over at my place frequently after that day. Every day, he would ask me new questions. For some strange reason, I never got tired of answering them. After a few weeks, he came up to me with a surprising request.

He bowed down.

"Please teach me to paint."

I scratched my head.

"I'm sorry?" I was trying to make sure I heard him correctly.

"I want to learn to create paintings like you."

"I don't think I'll be able to help you much."

"Why?"

I bit my lip slightly.

"I … I haven't painted anything for months." I confessed unequivocally.

"What? Why?"

"I don't know. I simply can't hold a brush anymore."

My heart sank when I uttered those words. Grisha noticed it and didn't question me any further. I grabbed my jacket and hurried towards the door.

"I'm going for a walk. If you want to paint, you can. Everything you need is in the studio."

I walked out while Grisha stayed put inside.

After I left, Grisha looked down at his hand. His hand had started to become transparent.

"Lumine, come on. Don't tell me all this now," he muttered.

When I came back, Grisha wasn't at home. He left a note saying he had left. He stopped coming home after this. I thought of calling him several times but something stopped me. I finally decided to visit him after a couple of weeks. I knocked at his door. There was no reply. I tried opening the door and found it unlocked. I slowly walked inside and was shocked to see Grisha lying unconscious on the floor. Looming above him was a canvas covered by a cloth.

"Grisha!"

I lifted him up and placed him on his bed. He seemed very light. Too light. Is he sick? I placed my hand on his forehead and found it cold. I shook him lightly.

"Grisha?"

His eyes slowly opened.

"Lumine? What're you doing here?"

"You didn't visit me for a long time. I was worried. What happened to you?"

"I'm just a bit exhausted. Don't worry."

My temper flared. I could sense something very wrong.

"Don't lie! You're ice cold and you don't weigh anything! What's happening!"

"Lumine, listen to me."

Something clicked in me. Grisha was never supposed to be able to see me. He would've continued living properly if he hadn't stopped before me. Was this happening because he strayed off his original life and walked into my world?

Grisha read my face and confirmed my suspicions with his eyes.

"Lumine, wait. I can explain."

"No. I shouldn't have spoken to you. I shouldn't have spent so much time with you. You should've just lived your life away from me." I sobbed.

I felt dizzy. My lungs stopped working properly. I was starting to hyperventilate. I got up and ran out of his house.

"Lumine!!"

GRISHA

After Lumine stormed out, I stayed in bed for a few minutes.

"Damn it."

I summoned my strength and got up. I grabbed the canvas and first went to Lumine's apartment. I placed it in the middle of her studio. I looked around the studio one last time. This small space contained so much happiness. It felt hard to move away from it. I exited the studio and started searching for Lumine. I roamed around the city for an hour before I leaned against a building, on the verge of collapse. Finally, I saw a figure standing atop one of the buildings. I remembered how she mentioned she would draw the scenery of the city from the top of the building. I ran towards the building.

LUMINE

I stood on the roof of the same building I once cherished. The beautiful and colourful scenery that I remembered was slowly being replaced by the dull grey colour that I hated so much. I couldn't stop thinking about Grisha. If he hadn't gotten involved with me, he might've lived. I regret meeting him and letting him get closer and closer to me. No. That's a lie. I don't have any regrets about meeting Grisha.

I heard the door slam open. Grisha stood at the door, panting heavily.

"I finally found you."

He fell down. I rushed to his side and cradled his head.

"Grisha!"

"Who makes a sick man run around the city for an entire hour?"

I looked away. He grabbed my face and stared at me.

"Did you mean everything you said back then?"

I started crying.

"I didn't. I can't say anything like that. I was so happy with you. I had so much fun."

He smiled.

"Thank god. This would be so much more awkward if you actually meant it."

As soon as he said those words, his body slowly started to fade.

"I wanted to let you know, I was also happy. I was so happy when I learnt all about colours and your world. I loved seeing it through your eyes."

His voice broke.

"I wanted to see more. I wanted to be with you more. I wanted to spend my life with you, Lumine."

My tears fell harder.

"Grisha …"

"Don't give up on painting. This world has begun to change because of you. More people will be able to experience what I did. I know it. Promise me you won't give up."

He slowly got up and looked me in the eyes. He kissed me. I managed to murmur a few endearing words between kisses before it was too late. As tears were streaming down his face, he slowly faded.

"Goodbye, Lumine." I heard a faint faraway voice one last time.

I sat there for a long time. I couldn't remember when at last I stopped crying. I got up in the middle of the night and walked back home. I entered my studio which seemed unnaturally quiet now. I saw a covered canvas in the middle of the studio. I wondered what it could've been. When I pulled off the cloth, my knees buckled. The entire studio exploded back into colour. The brightness of each colour was something I had never seen before. The studio glowed brightly. I tried to stop myself from crying again but I couldn't.

"Grisha …"

I sobbed loudly repeating his name again and again.

The painting was of a woman wearing a white dress with brightly coloured hair holding the hand of a boy who was stuck in a grey world. She was smiling happily.

I slowly wiped my tears and got up. I picked up Grisha's painting and hung it in the centre of the studio. I placed a new canvas on the easel and picked up my brush. My hand started moving on its own. As dawn started to break, I placed my new painting next to Grisha's and walked to the kitchen to get a cup of coffee.

In that painting was a woman with brightly coloured hair who was holding the hand of a man who was grinning widely while being surrounded in a world of colour.

Meanwhile in another part of the city, a small girl picked up a coloured crayon and started drawing on a piece of paper.

HI TO KORI

Ever since I could remember, Lena was always there with me. We'd spend every summer together. The two of us were born to two different kingdoms who were extremely close. Our fathers were almost like brothers. The two kingdoms prospered. When Lena and I were born, we both inherited the ancestral gift. I got the power of ice while she got fire. It was a rare inheritance for a chosen one. But somehow, we were chosen. My Mother, Ellyn, used to constantly be in the library reading all available records of the past wielders of magic in the family. The magic manifested gradually and would fully bloom when the user turns eighteen. Lena and I would often get sick due to the magic. Sometimes, our bodies are unable to keep up with the development of our magic. In my case, my body temperature decreases significantly and for Lena, it was the opposite. Whenever this happened, our mere presence was enough to treat each other.

As I grew up, my powers became stronger and more unstable. I stopped visiting Lena. I came to be known as the Glacial Prince. On my tenth birthday, my life changed. I ran away from my kingdom. I travelled around aimlessly. Most people identified me by my white hair and shunned me. I walked around in the rain for weeks. I never felt cold. I just felt empty.

Eight years passed. I was still somehow surviving and ended up in Lena's kingdom. I slept in alleyways. No one thought of robbing me and those who did ended up getting shattered into pieces of ice. I could sense some turmoil brewing in Lena's kingdom. I was somehow able to analyse the situation. There was a power struggle in the kingdom between the king and his general. The general was going to launch a coup and dethrone the king. Only one thing stood in his way. Lena. She had become very powerful, capable of taking out entire armies herself. But she was still untrained. Her powers weren't refined.

One day, I saw the royal guards approach me. They lifted their spears to my chest. I complied and followed them to the palace. The throne room opened and the king welcomed me with a weary face.

"It's been a while Tristan, the Glacial Prince."

"How have you been, Uncle?"

"Quite tired. You've had your ear to the ground haven't you, you should know why I'm tired."

"Why did you call me here, Uncle?" I looked at him straight. I was in no mood for riddles.

The king dismissed the guards and walked towards me.

"I need your help."

"How can I help you? I'm just a murderer." I shook my head frustrated.

"I know what actually happened, Tristan."

"I can't do anything for you, Uncle."

"It's Lena. Sadon is going to target her. He's going to kill her and overthrow me."

"This has nothing to do with me, Uncle. Please, Lena is way stronger than me. There's no way she can be taken down."

"She's naïve and inexperienced. She can't make it alone. She needs you. Please." Uncle's eyes were imploring.

"I'm sorry Uncle. I won't use my magic again. I'm going to avoid that curse." I stood firm in my decision and looked away.

I walked out before the king could speak again.

As I exited the palace, there was a commotion down the road. Citizens rushed up the road. I heard people talking of someone returning. I turned around and saw the king standing on his balcony looking at my receding figure.

I bit my lip and continued walking down the road, my cloak gently fluttering. I saw a huge escort slowly walk towards the palace. At the centre of the convoy was a red-haired lady on horseback. She had fair skin and her eyes were black. Her hair almost glowed in the sunlight. She waved at the citizens with a huge smile on her face. I heard the men next to me speak to each other.

"The princess is amazing. She dealt with a huge uprising all by herself."

"She will protect us from all the misfortune with her fire."

I looked down at my hands. It all just gets pushed onto us. I looked around and saw figures moving in the alleyway. I quickly scanned the entire area. After I finished, I stomped my foot. Red tendrils of ice slithered their way towards the figures. They were all caught in a mesh of fiery ice. One of them threw a dagger towards Lena. She was looking the other way.

I snapped my fingers and a small chunk of ice deflected the dagger. Her horse sensed the danger and whinnied loudly. Lena almost fell off from her horse. The convoy stopped and guards surrounded Lena. She looked around to see who could've attacked her. I put on my hood and covered my face. More daggers flew towards her. But this time, the guards protected her. The crowd ran for safety. I used the crowd and got closer to her. I snapped my fingers again and the guards were enveloped in ice. Lena turned to me and her eyes lit up in rage. I saw flames erupt from her hands. She directed it at me. I held out my palm and cancelled her magic. She looked shocked.

"Red ice! Who the hell are you!"

I walked closer and pulled her off the horse. The assassins slowly came out of the alleyway. Lena saw them and looked at me. One assassin flung another dagger at me. It ripped my hood.

"Tristan!"

I waved my palm across her face and put her to sleep. I caught her. I closed my eyes and saw a dark-haired lady walk towards me.

"Do you want me to deal with them?"

"Quickly."

I climbed the horse and I rode out of the city. Behind me were pieces of red ice and no sign of any assassins.

On the balcony of the palace, the king smiled.

"I knew you could never push her away," and the king was correct.

As I felt Lena leaning against me, I felt a little warm. Damn Uncle, he baited me perfectly. Sadon wants to kill Lena. But something felt off. It seemed like those assassins weren't there to kill her. They had plenty of opportunities. It was like they were there to capture her. What is he planning? I stopped near a creek. I lifted Lena and placed her under a tree. The horse merrily drank from the creek. I took off my cloak and covered Lena with it. I washed my face and cleaned myself. As I turned around, I felt a warm sensation. Lena was standing in front of me. Flames danced across her palm. She unleashed a wave of fire at me. I held my hands before it and my ice blocked it. The horse whinnied in fear.

"Are you really Tristan?"

"Do you know anyone else with white hair and uses magic?"

She slowly lowered her hand. I saw her lightly stagger.

"What are you doing, Tristan. Why did you kidnap me? Who were those people?"

Before I could answer, my entire vision went white. I saw a lady slowly approaching me. A lady with dark black hair.

"Not again."

The lady came closer and whispered in my ear.

"Why'd you kill me, Tristan?"

Red tendrils of ice coiled around my throat.

"WHY? WHY? WHY?"

Everything faded and I was back to reality. I was down on one knee and I was panting heavily. I felt sweat drip down my forehead. Lena walked closer anxiously.

"Are you ok?"

"I'm fine. Your father is being held hostage by Sadon. And he requested me to keep you safe."

Lena's eyes erupted in flames.

"He asked you! I'd rather be killed than be protected by a coward who ran away!"

I bit my lip. She wasn't wrong. Lena started to move towards the horse. I stood in her way.

"You can't go back. Not without knowing more about this situation. I won't let you."

Fiercer flames erupted from her hand.

"You think you can beat me?"

"I can't. Kill me and then leave."

I saw the hesitation in her eyes. She lowered her hand. She came closer and punched me on the face. I fell down. She pinned me to the ground. I felt tears fall on my face.

"Why did you leave? Why did you leave me alone for so long? I was in so much pain and I was so alone."

She sobbed lowering her head on my chest. I couldn't bring myself to console her.

"I hate you! I hate you."

I stayed silent. Watching her like this hurt but I couldn't console her. I didn't have that right.

Just then she collapsed.

"Lena?"

I tried to wake her up. I pushed aside her collar and saw a bright red mark.

"Shit."

She had overused her magic powers. She was trying to keep peace for eight years and she ended up using her magic constantly. I could've stopped this from happening.

I placed my hand on top of the mark. The mark became less bright. After a few minutes, Lena woke up.

"What happened?"

"You fainted."

I felt blood flow down my chin. I realized I was biting my lip too hard.

"You've been overusing your magic for quite some time, now, haven't you?"

"Whose fault do you think that is?"

I looked away as she got off me and stood up. I got up and tended to the horse.

"Don't use your magic anymore."

"What!"

"You heard me."

"I have to fight Sadon."

"You fainted because of a tiny flame. You can't fight anybody in your current state."

"So, I'm supposed to put my entire faith in you?"

"You don't have any other choice."

"I don't know if I can do that. I can't simply be watching from the side-lines."

"If you want to live, then don't use magic. I'll protect …"

I stopped my sentence midway.

"I'll fight them all."

"I will fight alongside you."

"I knew you would be very stubborn. I placed a seal on you."

Lena looked at me shocked.

"What!"

"You can't break out of the seal easily. You need lots of power for that. If you try to break it prematurely, you'll end up losing control and killing every living thing around you. So, you have to listen to me now."

She tried to punch me but I blocked it. Red fog slowly enveloped our hands.

"Why is your ice red?"

I felt my heart skip a beat for a second.

"It happened when I grew up."

I knew Lena didn't believe me but she decided to let it be.

"Where are we headed?"

"We're heading to a nearby village. I have a friend there who can give us more information."

I jumped onto the horse and helped Lena up.

It took an entire day to reach the town. It was around night-time when I found the inn. Lena and I walked into the inn which was also a tavern. Everyone immediately stopped and went silent when they saw me. A blonde-haired girl came running towards me.

"You made it."

"Keep your voice down, Juliana."

"How may I help you?"

"One room for the night."

"This way."

As Juliana turned around, four men blocked her path.

"There's no way we're letting a bastard like you stay here."

Lena stepped in front of me.

"What do you think …"

I grabbed her shoulder and pulled her back.

"I am not staying here tonight."

Lena turned around to me.

"What are you doing?"

"Stay close to Juliana. She'll give you everything you need."

"Don't fuck with me, Tristan. Why should I be the only one?"

I looked at her with hardened eyes.

"Leave this issue. Just stay here tonight."

As I was walking away from the tavern, I heard one of the men laugh and shout loudly.

"That's what happens to fuckers who kill their own mother."

I turned around and fog clouded my hands. I glared at him and he immediately looked away. I slowly walked away.

LENA

After Tristan walked away from the inn, I stood there speechless. I was finding it hard to breathe. That man mentioned something about Tristan killing his mother. Was there something more to his mother's death?

Juliana led me to my room.

"How do you know Tristan?"

"He saved me and got me a job here. The main innkeeper is also indebted to him. The innkeeper was constantly extorted. One day, the man came to him begging for forgiveness and repaid all the money he took. The Glacial Prince also paid us more than he was supposed to pay."

"Then shouldn't the innkeeper fight for him?"

Juliana looked down sadly.

"We both fought hard. But he told us not to. Forbade us. If it became known that the innkeeper supported the Glacial Prince, we would lose our lives and the inn would be burned down."

"I knew people blamed him but I didn't think they hated him this much."

"I don't believe the story. There's no way the prince killed his mother."

"Juliana, will you show me to the bath?"

"This way."

We both walked to the bathhouse. The bathhouse was huge. I undressed myself and entered the bath. All my fatigue disappeared. The warm water melted away all my thoughts and left me in a trance. I felt a chilly wind pass.

Tristan. What has happened to you? I noticed it before but I didn't want to admit it. His eyes seemed devoid of all life. It seemed empty. Like, there was no reason for him to live anymore.

That thought angered me. My body stiffened. Juliana touched my shoulder.

"Are you ok? What happened?"

I looked at Juliana and saw that her skin was red. The water around me was boiling.

"Oh no! Juliana, I am sorry."

Juliana smiled at me.

"I knew it was you."

"What?"

"Every time the prince came, there would be life in his eyes only when he talked about a princess with red hair. He used to keep saying that she would make him feel warm."

I couldn't say anything. He was thinking about me all this time? He actually missed me?

After we got out of the bath, Juliana looked at me.

"Please make the prince happy again."

I patted her head gently.

"You're a nice girl, Juliana."

She blushed. The two of us headed back to the inn. As soon as we entered the inn, there were a bunch of cloaked figures talking to the innkeeper. One of the men who didn't allow Tristan in was standing with them. He saw me and pointed at me.

"There. That's the one the Glacial Prince was with."

The cloaked figures looked at me. They came closer. One of them grabbed my wrist. I concentrated my magic at his hand. Nothing happened.

"Damn Tristan."

I tried to break free from his grip. Juliana tried to make him let go. The man slapped her and she fell down. My vision turned red. Red tendrils of ice made its way around his throat. He let go of my hand and clutched his throat. I rushed to Juliana.

"Are you ok?"

"Please run away from here."

The rest of the cloaked figures came closer. What did I do? How did I use Tristan's magic? I had to save Juliana. I tried to build up my power. I remembered what Tristan said and stopped. I looked at the door in desperation.

Just then, the door came crashing down and Tristan came through. He stomped his foot loudly and the figures were all encapsulated in red ice. The ice broke into several pieces. The man who tipped them off took a step back. Tristan turned to him. I saw pure, unfiltered rage in his eyes and enough killing intent to make a person nauseous.

"You hate me, fine. Come and kill me. You do anything that puts Lena in harm and I will make you beg for your death."

The man staggered and ran out the door. Tristan looked at me.

"Are you ok?"

His eyes were back to normal. That rage and killing intent. I never saw that in him. I never saw that much anger in one person. He helped Juliana up. A thin stream of blood flowed down her forehead.

Tristan walked over to the innkeeper.

"I'm sorry about this", he muttered and punched the innkeeper, suddenly. I ran to him and pushed him away.

"WHAT THE HELL ARE YOU DOING?" I chided Tristan.

The innkeeper smiled, surprisingly.

"You're too much, Prince. Please do what you have to. Don't worry. I'll take care of this mess. You take care of yourself, I beg you."

Tristan bowed, ready to leave. He turned to Juliana.

"I'll be back, Juliana."

"Take care, Tristan."

He took my hand and whistled. The horse came running towards us. As I turned around to look at Juliana and the innkeeper for one last time, the two of them smiled at us warmly. I knew that smile from was from the bottom of their hearts.

Then it all struck me. He punched the innkeeper so no one would suspect him of supporting the Glacial Prince. That way, he could still live with his business intact. As I saw Tristan on the horse, he somehow seemed taller.

I grabbed his hand and sat behind him. Ever since I met him again, the air around him was always cold. I leaned against his back. This time, it was warm.

TRISTAN

As Lena and I increased the distance from the inn, the scenery started to change. We passed through several green fields. Lena had fallen asleep and was leaning on me. I noticed that the mark I had on her had disappeared. I set it on her to make sure she could protect herself. Fortunately, it helped. I rode a little slower so as to not wake her up. As I was about to stop to let the horse rest for a while, a flying arrow suddenly pierced the horse. It shrieked and threw the both of us. I saw the horse whimpering. I clenched my fist and put it out of its misery. Lena sat up holding her head. She looked at the dead horse and gasped.

I immediately looked around to find the archer. Another arrow whizzed past my face. I looked at the direction it was fired from and found a cloaked figure like the ones back at the inn.

"More fucking shadows."

Lena came closer to me.

"I can't believe Sadon sent the shadows after me."

"He's really desperate for you."

I pushed Lena away as an arrow landed between us. A shadow dropped down and lunged at my throat with his dagger. I stopped it and froze his knife along with his hand. Before he could retaliate, Lena swept him off his feet and I killed him. The rest of the shadows materialized before us. I waved my hand at them. The tendrils of ice wrapped them all.

The ice melted before my eyes. I took a step back. What just happened? Lena was taken aback as well.

"My magic doesn't work."

I looked at their hands and saw a black bracelet. Was that protecting them? I aimed my magic at the bracelet. My ice melted again.

"You had something like this up your sleeve?"

The shadows lunged at me at the same time. I dodged the first blow, but the next ones cut me. The wounds weren't deep but I couldn't keep this up. I can't lose here. I won't lose.

I tried to use my magic again but I failed. One of them kicked me and I hit the tree. I tried to catch my breath. Lena lifted her hand and pointed at their bracelets. The bracelets cracked. The shadows were all surprised. I quickly jumped up and encased them all in ice. I slowly walked towards Lena and lifted her up. I looked down at my tunic and saw it was stained with blood.

Lena and I continued walking until we were safe. She sat me down under a tree and healed my wounds.

"What was with those bracelets?"

"Sadon must've come up with that to make you powerless."

"Why was only I able to break that?"

"Well, you're stronger than me. As painful as it, even when you're sealed, you're still more powerful."

That was a lie. Lena saw through my lie as well. Just then, my vision turned blurry. I felt my senses dull and I blacked out.

LENA

After I healed Tristan, I saw through his lie. He still didn't tell me how his magic changed. The colour of his magic always allured me. The bright blue ice. It was something I always adored. His new colour seemed too much like it was soaked in blood.

I saw his eyes droop. He tried to reach out and collapsed on my lap. "Tristan!"

I touched his face. It felt ice cold. I leaned down and brought my face close to his. I placed my hand on his cheek. I concentrated my magic and sent it to him.

This has happened before. When we were eight, I heard he had collapsed. His father immediately called for me. I rushed to his side and held his hand tightly throughout the night. The next morning, when I woke up, he was holding my hand tightly. He smiled at me.

"Thank you, Lena. For healing me and for not letting go."

I felt so happy when he smiled like that. It made me want to rush and be by his side no matter how difficult it was.

That same year, I had an extremely high fever. I was on the verge of death just like him. He came to me and saved me. When I woke up the next morning, I saw his eyes were puffy and red. When he saw me awake, he began to cry. He leaned against my head.

"I was so scared. I was scared that you would leave me."

"Don't cry. I'm fine now."

He wiped his tears and smiled at me. That same smile again. That one smile was something I wanted to protect so badly.

I concentrated all the magic I could muster. Stupid seal. I was slowly able to use more magic as the seal weakened. The colour slowly returned to his face. He opened his eyes.

"Lena?"

"What are you doing?"

"Remember that time when we were eight."

"I remember."

I saw a tear roll down his cheek.

"I can't live without you. I'm sorry I left you alone, Lena."

He placed his hand on my cheek.

"I'm sorry."

I felt a lump in my throat. I couldn't stay mad anymore.

"Still crying like back then."

He chuckled.

"And you can never seem to cry."

He sat up.

"I'll tell you everything. Everything that led up to this moment."

TRISTAN

I slowly recounted the events that made me who I am right now. Eight years ago, on my tenth birthday.

I remember Mom and Dad were running around excited for my birthday. The entire kingdom was lively with excitement. On my birthday, my Mom gifted me a beautiful blue cloak. She wrapped it around me and kissed my forehead.

"Happy Birthday, Tristan."

I thanked her and hugged her tightly. My Dad unveiled a bright ring. He slid it on my finger.

"This will protect you and everyone around you."

"Is it magical?"

"Yes. It's a special kind of magic."

My eyes lit up with awe. Soon, the day was over. My health slowly deteriorated. My hands were shaking uncontrollably. Blue mist was gathering around me. I felt my magic slowly take over me. I went up into my room and tried to close the door. I had a feeling my magic would boil over and something bad would happen. The mist intensified. Before I could lock the door, my Mother walked in.

"Tristan, what's wrong?"

I pushed her away.

"Don't come near me. Stay away."

I backed away from her. My magic overflowed and I lost control of it. Icicles formed around me. They were all pointed at me. I almost lost consciousness. The icicles hurtled at me in full speed.

I felt blood splatter all over my face. I felt a tingling sensation in my chest. I opened my eyes and saw a person embracing me tightly.

"Mother …"

She looked up at me. Blood poured out of her wounds. A stream of blood dripped down her chin. She stroked my hair gently.

"Tristan, you're very warm."

I held her tightly. She had enveloped me to protect me from the icicles. She sacrificed her life for me.

"Mother? Don't die!" I kept on sobbing uncontrollably.

She collapsed in my arms. I fell down to my knees. The icicles slowly turned red. The mist around me slowly disappeared. I sat next to my Mother, not able to stop crying.

Suddenly, she grabbed my throat.

"You should've been able to control your magic. I could've lived. I didn't have to die! Why did you kill me, Tristan?"

My father came rushing through the door.

"TRISTAN!"

He looked down at his queen and fell down to his knees, dismayed. He looked at me sorrowfully. My heart shattered. I left my Mom there in a trance and walked past my father. He tried to call out to me but I had already left. I grabbed the blue cloak I got as a gift and walked away. I walked and walked till my legs gave up. I lost track of time. I stared at my hands every now and then. The blood had dried. Red mist slowly emanated from my hands.

"This cursed magic. I won't let this same thing happen to Lena."

Just then my Mother walked towards me.

"You can't escape me. I will always haunt you."

I clutched my chest tightly and held back my tears. I got up shakily and continued walking.

Lena was silent for a while. She grabbed my shirt tightly. I saw her hands trembling. I smiled.

"You're too strong."

She looked at me surprised.

"You were always stronger. That's why I can rely on you."

She gripped it tighter.

"I'm sorry about everything I said when I met you."

I slowly got up.

"You were right. I was a coward. I killed my Mother and I simply ran away."

I looked into her eyes.

"I won't run anymore. I'll finish this properly."

We continued walking towards the next town. As we entered town, I walked into an alley.

"Tristan, where are you going?"

"I have a contact here."

As soon as I said it, a white-haired man appeared suddenly in front of me out of nowhere.

"Hello, Glacial Prince." He seemed to have sensed the purpose of our visit.

"Do you have what I had asked for?" I asked him urgently.

He held out his hand. I pulled out a bag of gold and dropped it in his hand.

"Sadon has left the kingdom. He's leading the shadows hunting for both of you."

Neither of us were surprised about it.

"Thanks for the information."

I stretched out my hand. He handed me a tattered scroll.

"It was very difficult to acquire."

"I knew you would be able to. Now leave."

He climbed the walls and jumped up onto the roof. Lena looked at me suspiciously.

"What is in that scroll?"

"It's something Sadon doesn't like. An important document."

There was a picture of a snowflake surrounded by flames on the scroll. Lena and I walked to a small restaurant. While she was eating, I opened the scroll and read it.

"What's in there?"

"Nothing that important."

"Will you tell me when you find something?"

"Sure."

She clicked her tongue. "I shouldn't trust you this much."

I smiled. I noticed her sad expression as well. I had a feeling she knew what this was about. I folded up the scroll and shoved it in my pocket. As we made our way out of the town, I saw cloaked figures surround us. A big, muscular man came forward. He had dark hair and he wore black armour. His eyes were menacing.

I stepped in front of Lena.

"Sadon."

All of the shadows had black bracelets with them. I looked at Lena. She nodded. Just then, a dagger flew past my face. It lightly cut my face and went through Lena's hair. I looked in front of me and saw Sadon's hand raised.

"I heard about it."

Before I could do anything, two shadows grabbed Lena. She tried to break out of their grasp. Before she could use her magic, they cuffed her with the black metal. Lena tried to escape but she couldn't.

The two shadows pushed her to the ground. Sadon slowly helped her up.

"It's a good thing you aren't strong enough to break the enchanted obsidian. The volcanic princess here was a great thorn in my side."

I bit my lip tightly.

"You're wondering why I'm so desperate for the princess aren't you?"

"I won't let you kill her."

"Kill her? I would never. All I want is her power. That destructive power. It can help bring peace. There is a war coming. I won't let any of my people die. In order to protect them, I'll gain this power."

Lena shouted at him.

"I will fight. You don't need to do this."

"Did you know your lifespan shortens when you use magic? You'll die if you keep using it. And if you die, how many more generations will it take before it is reborn. We don't know if it will even return."

I saw Lena's eyes waver.

"I want to protect my kingdom. I want to protect my father."

Sadon knelt down.

"If we can figure out your magic, we can make it so that it doesn't kill the people using it. We can then protect our kingdom, Lena. We can protect what's precious to the both of us."

"How can I trust you? What if you use it for evil?"

Sadon pulled out his sword. He cut his hand deeply. The blood dropped in front of Lena.

"I swear in the name of the King and my Honour, I will not use this power for any evil. I will only use it to protect my precious kingdom. That is my duty as the general of the army."

That was when I knew he was completely serious. Sadon would never fake a blood oath. He really wants to protect his kingdom. I looked at Lena's eyes. She had almost resigned.

"Then I will coopera …"

"I refuse." I cut in sharply.

Sadon turned to me. Lena looked at me in utter disbelief.

"Tristan, this can lead to peace. I can protect my father. I can protect all of them." She pleaded.

I don't want this. Years and years of torturing Lena. There's no painless way to extract magic. It's not so easy to dispel a curse. This cursed magic. I won't let it. I won't let it take Lena away from me. I'm done with magic. I won't lose anyone anymore.

I stomped my foot. Red tendrils of ice sprouted out around me. They all rushed to the nearest shadow. All of them melted instantly.

"It's time for your exit, Glacial Prince." Sadon's calm voice resonated.

The shadows all enclosed on me. I tried to dodge their daggers but I couldn't. The daggers dug deep into me. I tried to raise my hand but I couldn't. I heard my blood slowly drip. I was down on one knee. I saw Sadon pick up Lena and slowly walk away with her. Lena looked back at me with sad eyes.

"Goodbye."

No. Don't leave. Not you too.

My vision turned white. I saw my Mother slowly approaching me. Not this dream again. Not now. As usual, she came closer and closer. The closer she came, the harder it was for me to breathe. She clasped her hands around my throat. But I didn't feel anything. My Mother's face was always covered with a shadow. Her hands were usually lifeless.

But this time, it felt warm. Like Lena. Mother looked up at me. I could see her face. She let go of my throat.

"Tristan."

I felt a tear roll down my cheek.

"Mother."

"How long will you blame yourself?"

"But I killed you. If I could've controlled my magic. If I had acted fast enough, if I were stronger, I could've done something."

She placed a hand on my cheek.

"If I could go back to that moment, I wouldn't change anything."

"Mother."

"I've been trying to tell you something all this while."

I looked up at her.

"Your original colour is much prettier."

The tears fell harder.

She embraced me tightly.

"I'm sorry. I'm sorry."

"Don't blame yourself anymore. You have something important to do, don't you? Something you have to protect."

Lena …

Mother smiled.

"Show them your true power. Protect her with everything you have. I love you, Tristan. I will always be here to protect you."

Slowly, mist enveloped me. The red mist slowly turned blue. I'll move on. I won't let the guilt control me anymore. The red tendrils turned blue. The tendrils of ice wrapped itself around the obsidian bracelets. The bracelets shattered into pieces.

Sadon looked at me shocked. Lena gasped.

I slowly got up and stamped my foot. Everyone around me turned to ice. They were all knocked unconscious in an instant before they could react. This beautiful blue colour was Lena's favourite. This time, I'll finish it properly.

I slowly walked towards Sadon.

LENA

As Sadon was pulling me away, I looked at Tristan tearfully. But then, the air around him changed. The usual red mist turned blue. His magic had changed colours. It was not the one it looked like when he was a kid. It was a much more beautiful blue. I gasped in awe.

In the next instant, all the shadows collapsed unconscious.

Tristan …

TRISTAN

Sadon let go of Lena and walked towards me. He was wearing an enchanted obsidian armour. I won't be able to break that easily. And it had to be him wearing it. We squared off.

"Looks like you've become stronger now. Don't go underestimating me now."

I bit my lip tightly. I looked around for weak spots but I couldn't find any. Or even if I could, Sadon would've already made countermeasures. I tried to think several steps ahead but there was no scenario in which I could win. The only way I could win is if Lena and I team up. But I don't want to involve Lena anymore.

I made the first move and touched Sadon's shoulder. The ice immediately covered his shoulder. It shattered instantly. I dodged Sadon's blows but they were coming faster. He raised his fist and punched me hard in the abdomen. I quickly shielded the blow with a wall of ice before it hit me. I still staggered backwards. I sent two tendrils of ice below the ground towards his legs. I ran towards him. Before he could sidestep me, the tendrils grabbed his legs momentarily. Before they shattered, I was able to close the distance. I punched him across the face and sent him flying. He slowly got up and spat out a tooth. He came towards me. I channelled my magic to my hands. Lots of icicles formed behind me. But they all shattered instantly. I looked behind me in shock. Sadon smiled.

"Your magic becomes less and less effective against obsidian."

Shit. I was out of cards. Sadon kicked me in the stomach. I felt the wind rush out of me. He hit me with his foot again and again. He was heavily panting.

"Stay down, Glacial Prince."

I coughed up blood. My body was screaming in pain. I heard Lena scream my name. I slowly sat up. My knees were shaking uncontrollably. Lena was screaming at me.

"Please stop, Tristan! I don't want to see you getting hurt anymore."

I slowly inched one foot forward towards Sadon and Lena. Sadon looked at me shocked.

"Why do you keep coming back? Why do you want to save her so bad? This is what she wants. She chose this. What noble purpose are you trying to serve by saving her?"

I spoke quietly.

"I'm doing all this for myself. I don't have any noble or honourable cause. I don't want to let her go. I won't let her go. I won't leave her alone and I won't let her get hurt anymore."

"This can help save thousands of lives!"

"Maybe it can. But I won't stop protecting her. I won't let her face any pain alone."

Lena sat down shocked.

"You bastard. Your selfishness will lead my kingdom to ruin. I can't let this go on."

He punched me and I fell down. He unsheathed his sword.

"Farewell, Tristan."

He raised it and brought it down. But I never felt the steel pass through me. I felt the ground heating up. I looked at Lena and saw her aura increase in intensity.

"LENA!! NO!!"

Sadon stepped back.

"What is this!"

Lena looked at me.

"I won't let you get hurt in front of me, Tristan."

I felt the seal weaken. No! She'll end up killing everyone including herself. Sadon fell down to his knees. The obsidian was melting. I tried to get up to my feet. I slowly crawled towards Lena.

"Stop. Don't do it Lena. You'll die."

"Thank you for everything, Tristan."

She closed her eyes and the entire area was swallowed up in flames.

As my entire vision was taken over by flames, I barely finished concentrating. I felt the heat slowly subside. In front of me, Lena was covered in a block of ice. I felt my entire body writhe in pain. I looked down and saw my body completely burnt. I used whatever magic I could to heal the severe burns. My entire body was in agony. The ice melted and Lena fell down. I slowly got up. My legs couldn't take my entire weight. I fell to my knees several times before I was able to stand up. I looked around me.

There were no traces of life anywhere. Just then, I heard a groan. I walked over and saw Sadon slowly dying.

"My dream … my kingdom … I have to protect it."

I realized I was completely out of magic. I picked up the remains of a sword nearby and finished off Sadon. I closed his eyes. I walked over to Lena.

"I'll finish everything properly this time, Lena. I promise."

I kissed her forehead and slowly limped away.

LENA

I lost control of my emotions and I broke the seal forcefully. I lost consciousness. But before I lost consciousness, I felt very cold.

I slowly woke up. As I opened my eyes, I saw a barren charred area. It was around night-time. Did I do this?

I immediately clutched my heart. I'm still alive. How? I got up and walked around. I found Sadon.

I mourned for him for a minute. Everything that he did was for the sake of our kingdom. An honourable man.

I searched around and found no trace of anyone else. The weight of my actions hit me. I had used my magic to kill lots of people. I felt sick. Murdering my own countrymen in a peaceful time. I used all my strength to keep standing. I slowly walked around until I saw something that caught my eye. It was a piece of blue cloth.

Tristan!

I picked up the burnt piece of cloth. His cloak. Did I kill him?

No. No. I couldn't have. I cannot be the reason for his death.

"Tristan!"

I tripped and fell down.

"No. This can't be real."

I felt something touch my hand. I looked up and saw the scroll that Tristan was carrying. Much like the cloth, it too was almost burnt to ashes. I picked it up.

"How did this survive?"

I started to gain a little hope. Until I find his body, I will believe he is alive. He has to be nearby. I will find him. I got up with renewed vigour. I found a set of footprints.

"This has to be Tristan's footprints."

I snapped my fingers to create a flame. Nothing happened. I snapped my fingers again. What's happening? It should work. I snapped my fingers repeatedly.

"My magic is gone!"

Just then I saw a bright purple pillar of light shoot towards the sky.

"Tristan!"

I ran towards the light.

TRISTAN

That scroll. It had the story of how my predecessor made sure the magic would skip generations. It was considered bad not to pass on the magic to the next generation. But he didn't want his son to be burdened by the weight. He performed a certain ritual and sacrificed himself to stop the magic from passing onto the next generation. The scroll described the ritual. I memorized it instantly. But this curse. I don't want it to ever spread again. That's where I took a guess. If the person sacrifices his own power and soul, then it skips generations. What if you combined both fire and ice? Will that give me the result I want? Will that destroy magic?

Before Lena broke the seal, I absorbed all her power while keeping her safe. I ended up using most of my magic on her which made me unable to protect myself.

My body screamed in agony again as I thought about it. I raised both my hands and slowly drew the magic circle. As soon as I completed it, a pillar of light shot up into the sky. I stepped into the pillar of light. The pain increased immensely. My hands were trembling.

Blue mist enveloped my left hand while flames enveloped my right. I felt my life slowly fade away. I brought my hands together. Before I could combine them, I looked in front of me and saw Lena.

"What're you doing, Tristan?" her shriek rang through my quickly numbing ears.

I immediately lost my words. I saw a tear roll down her cheek.

She walked towards me slowly. She entered the circle and stood before me. She clutched my shirt tightly.

"Don't leave me."

She looked up at me with tears in her eyes.

"Don't leave me alone again. Don't go. Don't leave me. Stay with me."

She wrapped her arms around me and kissed me. I felt her warmth spread inside me gradually. A tender and gentle warmth.

"Let's go together."

Lena held my hands and the magic started converging at one point. The pillar of light started shrinking. It shrank into our palms and then exploded, spreading it all over the surrounding area. The burnt, desolate land slowly turned into a snowy field. Trees were covered in snow and bright red flowers bloomed around the field. In the centre of this field was a bright flame encased in a block of ice.

The two of us took in the beautiful sight and walked away together.

After a week, the two kings met up. Lena's father held up an envelope.

"I've been waiting for you to open this letter. One of Tristan's informants delivered this letter."

Father fidgeted uncomfortably.

Uncle read it aloud slowly.

"Dear Uncle, you planned this a long time ago, didn't you? You knew I would get involved if Lena was in danger. You're too smart sometimes. Thank you for giving me the opportunity to face myself. I won't run away anymore. And I won't let go of Lena. I'll be with her forever. Thank you, Uncle."

The enveloped contained another letter. Uncle handed it to Father.

"Father, I'm sorry for everything. I killed Mother and I ended up running away. I was scared. I was scared that you that something would happen to you as well. I missed you every day. I wanted to see you one more time. I'm sorry I never came back. I'm glad I was born of you. I love you, Father. Goodbye."

The king cried, his tears wetting the paper.

"I'm glad you were my son."

Uncle placed his hands gently on Father's shoulder.

After that, the magic never reappeared. In Lena's kingdom, people mourned her and she became the pride of the kingdom. Back in Father's kingdom, people's opinion of the Glacial Prince didn't change even when Father tried his best. In the end, he decided that it didn't matter. For him, the Glacial Prince was his pride and joy.

A few months later, the war happened. Uncle suffered lots of casualties until Father came to his aid and they together fought to win the war. The alliance between the two kingdoms was strengthened to even greater heights. Even though our magic would've shortened the duration of the war and reduced numerous casualties for both kingdoms, Uncle and Father pushed on ahead. For the sake of their children, they continued moving forward with their own power.

. . . .

CHIKARA

I slowly got up from bed. As soon as I stood up, a man walked in through the door.

"He has called for you."

I sighed and followed the messenger. We both stopped before an ordinary looking apartment. The messenger departed and I entered. A loud and boisterous voice echoed from deep inside the house.

"Is that you, Exia?"

"Yes. It's me."

A tall man with long blonde hair walked out of a room. He had a bright smile and an overbearing personality.

"I'm so glad to see you. It's been so long."

"You saw me just yesterday." I retorted incredulously.

"It feels like an eternity when you're away from me."

"Just give me my assignment." I was impatient.

"Ah! The same as usual. I've already done the preparations. You just need to travel."

"This stupid thing over and over again. I'm sick of it."

"This one might surprise you."

"I doubt it."

"I believe in him. I believe he'll change you as well."

"It's rare to see you vouch for someone."

"This person is quite interesting."

I furrowed my brows. How different can he be? This is going to be another short experiment. I sighed and packed up my bags. I walked out of my house and saw the golden portal shimmering. I walked through it. I reached the edge of a town. According to him, I was looking for a doctor. I slowly walked into a town.

DOCTOR

As I was preparing my files and opening my clinic, a golden circle appeared in front of me. A tall blond man appeared through it. I jumped back. The man laughed loudly.

"Don't worry. I'm not here to hurt you."
I pulled my cheeks tightly.
"That hurts. So, it's not a dream."
I walked up to him and pulled his cheeks hard.
"Ow! What the hell are you doing?"
"I mean, you could be an illusion."
"I'm real! That really hurt!"
"Sorry about that. So how may I help you?"
"Why did you open this clinic?"
I stared at him weirdly.
"Because I want to help people. I don't like pain, you see."
"Interesting. What if I told you I had a power that could help you save lots of people?"
"I'd want it."
"Even if it has very serious repercussions. Like your death?"
I scratched my chin.
"Can I save lots of people in exchange for my life?"
"You can but it won't be an easy death."
"Then I'd want it."
The man laughed.
"You might just be the one. You're stupid enough."
"Who're you calling stupid!"
The man stretched his hand out and placed it on my chest.
"I hope you'll be able to achieve your dream with this."
I felt a warm sensation course through my body. After a few minutes, it stopped.
"What power is this?"
"That would ruin the fun. Feel free to use that power however you want."
His eyes turned cold.
"But if you use it to harm someone else, you will die a horrible death in my hands."
I stepped forward.

"I'm assuming you already know everything about me. You should know the chances of that happening."

He gave a sudden laugh.

"That was just a polite alert. I know everything about you, so I'm not worried. Take care."

He slowly started walking back to the portal again.

"Oh, by the way, one of my subordinates is coming to assist you in your endeavours. Please take care of her as well."

"Wait wha ..." My sentence remained unfinished.

He went through the portal and disappeared.

A subordinate? Who is going to come now?

I opened my clinic and just worked. There weren't a lot of people who came in usually. Around evening, someone walked in. It was a dark blue haired girl with black eyes. Her hair went down till her waist. She had a halo above her head.

"Ah! You're the doctor."

"You must be the subordinate he talked about."

"I'm Exia. Nice to meet you."

"Nice to meet you, too."

I looked at her luggage. I took it from her.

"This way."

I walked upstairs and placed the bags in the spare room.

"It's not much but I hope you'll be fine with it."

"It's fine. Thank you."

"So, are you here to monitor me?"

"And also to help you. I have some medical expertise."

"That's a relief."

Just then, I heard the door open. I walked downstairs. A woman entered carrying her son into the clinic.

"Doctor! Please help him!"

"What happened?"

"He got hit by a carriage."

The boy was bleeding profusely. I helped to set him down on the table. I checked his pulse which was slowing down gradually. I looked down at his injuries. No. No. I think I can't save him now. I can't do anything, it's too late. But I need to do something. I need to be stronger. I need to save this boy!

Just then, I felt a warm sensation course through my body. Suddenly, the warmth turned to an ice-cold sensation. I felt it constrict my heart. But the boy. I checked his pulse and saw that it was stable. I immediately started treating him. I finished attending him and sat down slowly. Exia was finishing up the procedure.

"He'll live."

The woman looked at me with tears in her eyes.

"Thank you so much, Doctor."

How did that happen? He should've died. I shouldn't have been able to save him. Was it because of that power?

As I slowly walked upstairs to ask Exia about it, I coughed out blood. I buckled on my knees. Exia came rushing upstairs.

"You used that power, didn't you? There's no way he should've lived."

I kept on coughing blood. The pain racked my entire body. My hands were trembling slightly. But the pain gradually started fading.

"Are you ok, Doctor?"

I chuckled.

"So, I really can save people!" I looked at my hands incredulously.

I laughed. Exia looked at me concerned.

"I can do this. I can save people."

I laughed harder while Exia looked at me even more concerned.

"Doctor!"

"I will make up for my past this time."

The pain completely disappeared the next day. I woke up feeling normal. As I opened my door, I saw Exia walk out of her room.

"Morning!"

"Good morning! How are you feeling?"

"Feeling normal. Time to work some more."

"Don't push yourself too much."

"You've started caring about me knowing me merely a day!"

"I don't want good people to die."

I looked down and murmured.

"A good person? Heh …!"

"What?"

"Nothing. Let's eat."

I prepared breakfast quickly. Exia sat down and ate slowly.

"This is very tasty." She said after gulping down a portion.

"Yeah, I can tell it from your expressionless face."

She got up and walked to the kitchen and started rummaging through the cupboards. She took out the bottle of chilli powder.

"Exia, what are you doing?"

"Put some of this."

I got up and slammed the table.

"I'll die if I eat that, woman."

Before I could react, she sprinkled it on my plate. I looked down in horror. She stared at me intently.

"Eat now."

I shakily picked up the spoon and brought it to my mouth. As I swallowed it, I was surprised. It actually tasted better. Exia went and added it to her plate as well.

"This is much better now. Are you also a cook?"

"I live alone, so I had to learn cooking."

"Exia, you're amazing. Cook for me from now on."

She gave me a blank stare.

"Ok."

We both finished our breakfasts and started prepping the clinic. As soon as we finished, a woman walked in with a basket.

"Oh, hello. How's your son doing?"

"I've been doing everything you asked me to do, Doctor."

"Then, he'll be fine. There's nothing to worry."

She handed over the basket to me.

"It's just a token of appreciation. I'm so grateful to you, Doctor."

"Oh, thank you. But you don't need to do this. I'm this town's doctor. It's my job to help those who are in pain."

The woman thanked me once more before she left. I looked into the basket and saw bright red apples.

"Exia! Come here!"

Exia walked over slowly.

"It's so beautiful."

I felt a tear forming.

"Please make something for me with this."

"Just felt you should know; I didn't come here to cook for you."

"Then you shouldn't have shown me your true skills. Mark my words, Exia. I will make you want to cook something for me!"

"I accept your challenge."

"You and your blank face. Can't you smile?"

Exia lifted her hands to her face and pulled her cheeks.

"Like this?"

"Never mind. That is another task I will accomplish eventually."

Exia took the basket from my hands and walked away with her same expressionless face.

I chuckled. When was the last time I saw such a beauty? I mean, I did look at myself yesterday in the mirror but it's been a long time.

I got a phone call in the afternoon. I put down the phone and walked up to Exia.

"We've got to go and pick up some medical supplies. Tell me when you're ready."

After half an hour, we both left the clinic and walked a few miles to the merchant. When we arrived, he was shouting orders at people. The entire area was flurrying with activity. As soon as he saw me, his eyes lit up.

"Doctor, it's been a long time. Here are the things you need."

He handed me a big crate. I almost dropped it when I received it.

"That's heavy."

"Did you forget how much you ordered?"

"Well, I didn't expect it to be this heavy."

Just then, Exia lifted it out of my hands with ease. I felt heat rise up my cheeks. The merchant laughed loudly.

"You've got yourself a great assistant, Doctor."

I turned to Exia.

"Exia! Don't embarrass me like this."

"You looked like you needed my help carrying this."

I felt my face go apple red.

"Let's go quickly." I hurried off.

I waved at the merchant and we headed back to the clinic. Once we reached the clinic, there were people waiting outside. In fact, the entire town was on the streets. I asked Exia to go ahead and store the supplies. I called one of the people and asked what's going on.

"The military is coming back home."

"Already?"

"I heard that they're all preparing for war."

A war. There have been frequent skirmishes with the neighbouring country. Could it actually have led to a war?

My hands were trembling before I realized it. Another war? Was this retribution? Maybe this is the chance for me to make up for everything I did wrong. I touched my chest. With this new power, maybe I can make up for what I did.

The sounds of horses woke me up from my thoughts. I walked into the clinic and started preparing for all the wounded that were about to come in. As I expected, I heard the door open and several soldiers walk in. A man came and walked up to me. He had long black hair and his blue eyes were filled with only battles and survival.

"Doctor, please take care of my men."

"Ah, Commander, welcome back home."

The Commander looked behind me.

"New assistant?"

"Yes. She's a total beauty. And she cooks very well."

The Commander chuckled.

"I see. Let us have a drink after you're done."

"See you at the usual place."

I turned my attention to the injured soldiers. Exia and I tended to them throughout the evening. After finishing the treatment of the last solider, I collapsed into my seat in exhaustion.

"Good work today, Exia. You can take a break tomorrow."

"I can still work."

"Oh, I know. But I want you to go outside and explore as well. Hey, you don't know this place well, do you? Ok. I've decided. I'll show you around our town."

I turned around to see her reaction and I saw her blank expression. This time, she realized it and pulled her cheeks to smile. I chuckled.

Maybe tomorrow is going to be a good day.

After we finished dinner, Exia and I washed the dishes. After washing, I cleaned up and started getting ready. Exia yawned.

"I'm going to bed. Tomorrow is going to be a long day."

"Don't make it sound as if its bothersome."

She turned around slowly.

"I'm looking forward to it."

I was caught off-guard by her response.

"Don't end up drinking too much."

I waved goodbye and walked towards the bar. The bar was empty. The bartender waved at me and started preparing my drink. I sat down next to the Commander.

"You look awfully happy."

I grinned.

"Got myself a date."

"I can't tell if you seriously like her or not."

"Suspense is good."

The Commander chuckled. The bartender placed my drink in front of me. I picked it up and sipped it slowly.

"Been a while since we sat down like this."

"The situation isn't good. The skirmishes are slowly escalating."

"Another war?"

"Seems that way. Maybe a month or less. The government has already finalized battle plans."

I looked down at my drink.

"Another reminder, eh? Fate is either messing with me or giving me another chance."

"You didn't do anything wrong that time. Nobody blames you."

"It doesn't justify it, does it now?"

I finished my drink.

"This time, I won't run away. I'll stand my ground. I won't avert my eyes anymore."

The Commander looked at me worriedly.

"I'll see you at the battlefield, old friend."

I left the bar and walked back to the clinic. I clenched my fists tightly. I remembered all their faces. I walked into my room and closed my eyes.

EXIA

I saw so many people fail using this power. They all gave up after their first try. The pain was too much to handle. I didn't blame them or resent them. I could understand why they would quit. Everyone had good intentions, but none of them could take the process forward to its conclusion.

My first assignment, I was naïve. I believed in the strength of others and believed that they would be able to use this power properly. But each and every time I saw their pain, my belief started eroding. I couldn't bear to see all these people in pain. Most of them never recovered from the pain. They lost their minds and could no longer live normally.

This cursed power. I wanted nothing more than to destroy it. But soon, after countless people, I stopped feeling. I didn't feel anything when I saw people shatter. I stopped thinking about others. Just simply standing beside them lifeless. I wanted someone to break this power.

To make sure this stops. That's what I wanted. But the power was too much for a human to break. I tried several times to destroy it myself but I couldn't. This power that shattered my heart, I want it to burn.

Then, when I met the Doctor for the first time, there was something different about him. Behind his bright smile, was complete darkness. I knew he had some kind of trauma. I didn't think he'd be able to survive the first attempt. When he used the power and saved that boy's life, he started laughing. I thought the power had driven him insane and I was ready to remove it. But when I looked into his eyes, I saw clear determination. I saw fire. A growing fire.

When he woke up the next day, I didn't see any signs of stress on his body. I found him. I found the person who can shatter this power. The person who can save me. I started believing in him. Every day, I spent working with him, I felt my spirits rise. I slowly regained my emotions. He slowly pieced my heart together. I realized I had fallen in love with him.

When he said he would show me around the town, I felt happy for the first time. But I couldn't smile properly yet. That night, when I went to my room, I stood in front of the mirror. I tried to smile naturally but it didn't work. I spent an hour trying to smile before collapsing on my bed without any luck. I closed my eyes and waited for the next day.

DOCTOR

I woke up as soon as the sun's rays filtered in. I walked out of my room and saw Exia dressed up. She wore her white coat over her normal clothes. Her hair was let down and her halo glowed brightly.

"I forgot to ask, is your halo only visible to me?"

"Yes. Does it look weird?"

"It looks good. I'm loving the entire angel cosplay. But is it a cosplay if you really are an angel? Now this is a really good question. Hmm …"

Exia blushed. I rubbed my eyes and looked closer.

"Did you just blush right now?"

As soon as I said it, she turned around. Her face returned to normal.

"I don't know what you're talking about."

I laughed.

"Shall we start our sightseeing?"

We walked down the stairs and walked out. The weather was beautiful today.

"Where would you like to go to first?"

"Aren't you the guide?"

"Well, there's not exactly a lot in this town. Its main charm is the homely vibe."

I snapped my fingers.

"Ah, I know exactly where to go."

I grabbed her hand and walked towards the playground. I didn't need to look behind me to tell that she was blushing as I held her hand. We reached the playground. I checked my watch and nodded.

"Doctor, why did you bring me here?"

"You'll see."

A few minutes later, a lot of children came running towards me.

"The doctor is here!"

I knelt down. All the kids jumped on me and took me down. They all wrestled with me and plastered me to the floor. Exia looked at me nervously.

"What's wrong?"

"I've never been around kids."

I laughed and got up.

"Hey guys, I brought someone with me today. I hope you can show her this town."

All the kids turned to Exia. They all cheered loudly. A little girl walked up to Exia and tugged at her coat.

"You're very pretty. Are you the Doctor's wife?"

I heard everyone else gasp.

"The Doctor is married?"

I held my hand over my mouth to stop myself from laughing.

"No, no! The Doctor is just my boss."

Another kid immediately pointed at Exia.

"Ah, she's blushing."

Exia immediately looked away. I looked at her closely.

Just as I thought, you were bearing all the pain alone behind your expressionless face. You don't need to shoulder it alone. I'll bear it with you for the rest of my life. However short it will be.

The children slowly took Exia around the town. Another little girl walked towards me holding something behind her back. She gave it to me. It was a blue flower. The same colour as her hair.

"It's for her."

"Why don't you give it yourself?"

"I want you to give it to her."

I smiled and lifted her up.

"Thank you for the assist."

The little girl laughed and slowly ran towards Exia.

EXIA

The kids swarmed around me and showed me every part of the town. All the townspeople referred to me as the "Doctor's wife" which made me blush constantly. After exploring the town, everyone swarmed around me and bombarded me with questions. I tried to keep up with them and answer all the questions but I couldn't.

They all smiled joyfully. I cherished their smiles. It warmed my heart. I wanted to be able to smile like this for the Doctor.

The sun started setting and all the children went home. I waved at them and walked back to the playground. The Doctor was sleeping on the bench.

I sat down and placed his head on my lap. I gently stroked his hair. I looked down at his hands and saw him clutching a blue flower tightly. Was it meant for me? I felt the warm sensation pulsing through my body. I took the flower and placed it over my heart. I smiled naturally.

DOCTOR

The declaration of war came a few days later. The armies marched constantly. Our village was also in the process of evacuation since we were at the edge of the country. The Commander was placed in charge of our town.

"Exia, you can leave with the villagers. Keep them safe."

"I can fight."

"I don't doubt it. But it's going to be ugly."

"I've seen several wars. I'm much older than you."

I chuckled.

"And I don't want to leave you alone."

I looked at her. My heart sped up a little. No. There's no way she meant it that way.

"Ok. You're going to help me here then."

The border was just a few miles away so I decided to set a medical camp in the town.

"Let's go get ready."

Just then, the door opened and a young girl walked in. She had long black hair and her glasses were almost about to fall off. She was carrying a huge box.

"I'm back, Doctor."

"Ah, Jessica. Welcome back."

I rushed over and took the box.

"Did you finish your learning?"

"I did."

"Good. You're going to have to apply everything now."

I saw her forehead beaded with sweat.

"It'll be fine, Jessica. Exia and I will protect you and make sure you're alright."

"Exia?"

Jessica looked behind me and jumped up.

"Oh, sorry about that. I'm Jessica, the Doctor's junior."

She came closer to me.

"I didn't know you were the romantic type."

"Hey! She's my assistant, Jessica. She's quite skilled as well, so you can approach her any time."

Exia extended her hand.

"Nice to meet you."

"She's so pretty, Doctor."

"I know."

"Jessica is going to inherit the clinic from me."

"So much pressure!"

I placed my hand on her head.

"You'll do great. I'm sure."

Jessica nodded.

"I'll do my best."

"That's the spirit. Now help Exia out. I have to go meet the Commander."

EXIA

After the Doctor left, Jessica and I were alone.

"So have you known the Doctor for a long time?"

"I met him a few years ago when he had just set up this clinic. He found me one day, studying outside his clinic. When he saw I had a book on medicine, he took me into his clinic and taught me personally.

I ended up acing my classes and became the best student. I came to the clinic every day and stayed here throughout the day. A year ago, he sent me outside the town to learn from a very famous medicinal school."

"And you just came back."

"Yes. What about you? It's rare to see the Doctor acknowledge someone as skilled."

"Well, I have a lot of experience on the battlefield."

"Oh, just like the Doctor?"

"The Doctor?"

Jessica turned away.

"Oh, you don't know."

"What are you saying?"

"If he didn't tell you, then he must have a good reason."

I looked at Jessica pleadingly.

"Tell me about him."

"I don't know much. But I knew he was a great doctor in the army. People in this town almost revered him. Even in the military, he was loved and respected by everyone. The Commander was his closest friend. He will know more."

"Sorry, Jessica. Can you take care of this alone for some time?"

"Ah … mmm … wait …"

I ran out before Jessica could complete.

"Ah, I'm going to be in so much trouble."

I ran around town until I found the Commander. He was giving orders and dispatching soldiers. After he finished, he turned to me.

"The doctor's assistant, Exia was it?"

"Yes. I have something I want to ask you."

The Commander and I stepped away and sat down on a bench.

"The Doctor's past? Well, it's not a rosy one. But before that, may I know why?"

"I can see through his fake smiles. I know there's something on his mind constantly. There's something that's hurting him every second."

"That is true. It hurts me as well to see him like this. The Doctor and I served together in the military for a while. Every soldier was able to fight their hardest because they knew they had a great doctor on whom they could depend, and the Doctor never let one of them down.

There was a big war years ago. Much like this one. We were sent to a particular town that had no time to evacuate. The Doctor had to stay in that town while my men and I fought outside it. But the battle involved the entire town as well. Civilians and soldiers were all indiscriminately butchered. The Doctor managed to save people as best he could.

A little boy was brought to him, severely injured. He tried to save him for hours and hours but he failed. When his mother found out, she committed suicide in front of the Doctor. We learnt after the war that the father who was a soldier had also perished. When I came back to the city at the end of the day to get my injuries healed, I saw the Doctor kneeling before the two corpses. His clothes were all bloody. That was the first time I had seen him cry. He couldn't take it anymore. He left the army.

Not a single soldier blamed him for leaving. He had saved so many lives in that war. But he blamed himself. Thought he was a coward for leaving the war. After the war ended, I couldn't find him. A year later, he came back to that very same town and opened a clinic. The people remembered everything he did for them and welcomed him with open arms."

"This was that town?"

"Yes. And now this town is again forced to suffer through this. But I didn't want a repeat of history. So, I finished evacuating the village. The blood of those people is on my hands as well."

"So, this is why the Doctor is hurting?"

My chest was hurting. I didn't want the Doctor to feel like this. I wouldn't let him feel this way. I'll get rid of his pain. I won't let him suffer anymore.

I thanked the Commander and walked back to the clinic. I saw the last of the townspeople leaving the town. They were loading the carriages. I decided to help them when I saw the Doctor come and help them load. A little girl was crying. The doctor bent down.

"What's wrong, Dear?"

He looked at her finger and saw that it was bleeding. He pulled out a small piece of cloth from his pocket. He wrapped the girl's finger.

"There. Now it's alright."

She slowly stopped crying,

"Are you not coming with us?"

"I have to stay here and make sure everyone is ok."

"Will you be waiting here?"

I saw the Doctor hesitate. He bit his lip. He never answered her question. Her parents came and they climbed the carriage and slowly left. He turned around and saw me.

"Welcome back."

Again, that fake smile. I felt my chest tighten.

"Doctor … I want to talk to you."

The Doctor turned around and looked at me intently.

"What do you want to talk about?"

"I heard about what happened to you in the past."

His face darkened.

"What about it?"

"You're still hurting from it aren't you?"

The Doctor didn't respond.

"You did everything you could. You tried your best …"

"Stop."

My sentence was left incomplete. I lost all my words. The Doctor stared at me coldly.

"Don't say anything like that. I didn't try or help anyone."

"That's not true …" I tried to reason.

"Two thousand men."

"What?"

"Two thousand men died after I ran away. I could've saved them all. But I didn't. I went to apologize to all of their families but surprisingly I didn't see a hint of anger or resentment in them for me."

I was speechless.

"I got their husbands and sons killed and not one of them blamed me! I wanted nothing more than to shout at them. But I couldn't. No matter where I went, no one would chastise me. They all think I did what I could."

The Doctor looked at me, his eyes filled with pain. I felt my heart crack. Don't make that face.

"Don't show me any more kindness, Exia."

Seeing Doctor's painful expression, I felt like leaving everything and running away. I thought I was adding to his grief. But I couldn't bring myself to leave him alone.

"Then let me share your burden."

"What?"

"Don't bear it on your own. Lean on me."

"I don't want to involve you in this."

I clenched my fists tightly. I grabbed his collar and slapped him tightly. I felt a tear drop. All the anger subsided instantly.

"You're so unfair, Doctor. Doing so much for me and helping me and then you say that. You're not the only one suffering because of this. Seeing you like this …" I couldn't complete the sentence.

I walked away.

DOCTOR

After Exia slapped me and walked away, I stood there silently. I touched my cheek. It hurt more than what a normal slap would. I just made her cry. What the hell am I doing?

I slapped myself again. I slowly regained my focus. How long will I be dwelling on the past? She's hurt now because of me. Because I can't let go of the past. I will let go of everything except her.

"I will leave everything behind in order to protect her."

Just then, a soldier walked towards me.

"The Commander is calling for you."

I followed the soldier and met the Commander.

"How are the preparations?"

The Commander looked at my bright red cheek.

"Lover's quarrel?"

"Just a wakeup call that I might have needed."

The Commander looked at me surprised. My eyes were filled with renewed vigour.

The Commander smiled at me as he briefed me on the plans. I helped him out with the strategy and we finished our talk in around night.

"The battle is very close. Stay well rested."

The Commander patted me on the shoulder.

"You get some rest as well. Go fix your problems first."

I slowly jogged back to the clinic. I opened the door and found Jessica washing the dishes.

"Doctor, welcome back."

"Where's Exia?"

"She said she was going out for some air."

"Thanks, Jessica."

I slowly walked towards the playground. I found Exia sitting on the bench. She looked at me coming.

"How did you know I was here?"

"It's not exactly a big town. And I know this place is special to you. I mean this is where we had our date."

"I'm not in the mood for your jokes right now, Doctor. If you don't have anything to say, I'll just leave."

She got up and slowly started walking towards the clinic. I grabbed her hand.

"Doctor?"

I pulled her closer and hugged her tightly.

"You were right. I wasn't the only one hurting back there. I'll stop living in the past. It might take some time but I'll try my best. I don't want to see your tears again."

"What are you saying?"

"Please allow me to lean on you. I can't save myself on my own."

Exia slowly wrapped her arms around me.

"Lean on me as much as you need to. I will be with you every step of the way."

That one moment felt blissful. I wanted it to last forever. Embracing the one I love. That's the ending I wanted.

A week later, the war started.

I somehow managed to hide all the pain from Exia. I leaned against the tree, every part of my body screaming in agony. I felt my mind slowly melt.

"I've reached my breaking point."

I felt that cold sensation grip my heart strongly. There were injuries … and I was busy keeping death away even from fatal ones …

How many deaths did I thwart? I lost count after fifty. I was slowly getting weaker with each passing life giving, I felt myself nearing my own end. That day … it was the fifteenth day of the war … I felt a bit more numb than usual. After my morning round, I came back to my tent. If I were to faint now, I most probably would not wake up again. My knees started to buckle. Before I collapsed, I saw Exia walk towards me. No. I won't collapse in front of her. I won't die yet. I haven't even seen her smile yet.

I chuckled softly. I gathered all my strength and faced Exia. I managed to send her away to do my rounds. I knew I couldn't hold on anymore. I slowly closed my eyes. The only thing I could see was Exia. Her blank expressionless face. It somehow made me happy. But I wanted to see her smile once.

As I opened my eyes again, I saw Exia rush towards me. I smiled at her before my vision blurred and my head hit the ground.

EXIA

I shouted for help.

"Doctor! Stay with me!"

A few soldiers came running towards me. They helped me carry the Doctor to his office. I instructed one of the soldiers to quickly bring Jessica. Jessica was out of breath when she entered the office. Her eyes widened in horror when she saw the Doctor.

"What happened!"

"I'll explain later. He's lost a lot of blood. We have to save him now!"

I saw a new side of Jessica at that moment. She wasn't the shy or nervous Jessica anymore. Her eyes darted across the body of the Doctor and she immediately knew what to do. She worked quickly and efficiently. I helped her. After hours, Jessica stopped working.

"We've stopped the bleeding."

I looked at her relieved. Jessica looked at me with tears in her eyes.

"It's going to take a miracle for him to wake up again."

I lost all my strength. I sagged onto the chair. No. This can't be happening. Doctor. Jessica walked out to tend to the soldiers. I leaned on the Doctor's chest. I pounded on it lightly.

"Why? Why did you do it? I can't bear to see you like this. It hurts. Wake up and take my pain away."

The tears were slowly soaking into his bloodstained shirt.

"Doctor!"

A week passed. I knew I should've been out there helping Jessica but my legs wouldn't move. I was scared to leave. I wasn't able to stop my tears.

I stayed by the Doctor's side constantly. I lost track of time until I felt something touch my hair. I slowly got up and saw his hand on my head.

"Doctor?"

"Good morning."

The tears fell with renewed vigour. I hugged him tightly.

"I was so scared!"

He pulled me close and held me.

"I'm not done yet. I can't leave without seeing your smile."

I couldn't hide my surprise. The Doctor laughed.

"That's a new expression."

My smile? If I knew how to do that, I would've done it. I would smile constantly for him.

The Doctor tried to get up. He groaned and slumped back into the bed.

"What are you doing!"

He looked at me with gentle eyes.

"How long has it been?"

"You've been unconscious for a week."

"The war is still raging on, isn't it?"

"I don't care about that! Right now, you need to rest!"

"Exia, we are still at war. I've had enough rest."

I clenched my fists tightly.

"What are you talking about?! LOOK AT YOU! You can barely stand up! You can't help anyone like this!"

"Are you sure?"

"You're going to continue using that power?!"

The Doctor chuckled.

"You're suffering so much. Why are you still continuing?"

"It's because I have the power to save people. It's a disgrace if I don't use it properly."

I tried to hold him down.

"Stop, please. I can't bear to see you in any more pain. It hurts me."

The Doctor sat up. He leaned against me.

"I have to, Exia. I want to do this. I want to use this power."

"You can't even move."

"Then help me."

I looked at him shocked. He extended his hand.

I wiped my tears.

"Why do I agree to all of your stupid ideas?"

The Doctor laughed loudly.

"Hey, only some of my ideas are stupid."

I slowly supported him and helped him up. He put his arm around me and we slowly walked outside.

Every soldier stood shell-shocked as they saw the two of us walking. The Doctor waved at everyone. Once we reached the centre of the camp, every single wounded soldier sat up and looked at the Doctor.

They all sat silently. Every single person stood silently with immense respect. Jessica rushed over to us.

"Doctor! What are you doing here?!"

"Hey. Just here to do my job."

"Look at you!"

"Good job, Jessica. I knew I could place my life in your hands."

His eyes shone with genuine gratitude.

"You have already surpassed me. I'm proud of you."

Tears formed in Jessica's eyes.

"Doctor …"

"Now, let's get back to work shall we."

I saw him glow slightly. Was that his power? The light around him subsided. Suddenly, the Doctor was able to move without my help. I saw his face contort in intense pain. But he continued walking towards the camp. Even though the Doctor was in immense pain, he was still able to work. He was able to keep up with Jessica and the other doctors. He didn't falter or stop moving. Sometimes, in between, he would be unable to hold anything. I saw the pain in his eyes. I walked over to him but he waved his hand at me. He smiled.

How was he able to smile? Even through so much pain and misery. How is he still smiling?

At the end of the day, Jessica and the other doctors managed to persuade the Doctor to take rest. The Doctor conceded and called for me.

"I can walk on my own now."

"I don't want you to overexert yourself. Your injuries are still life threatening."

The Doctor smiled sadly.

"Life threatening, eh!"

"How are you still able to smile? I know how much pain you're in. But you're still able to smile. How?"

"How? It's because I'm thinking of a beautiful blue haired girl with a halo above her head. She gives me strength and makes me want to continue working hard."

"Doctor … It's the same for me! You're my source of strength."

The Doctor looked at me surprised.

"Exia!"

A soldier ran up to the both of us.

"The Commander has successfully taken down the enemy catapult. He is currently charging into their backline with the reinforcements flanking the enemy."

"Good news."

"But we suffered lots of casualties. They're all flooding into our camp. The doctors from the other battalions will only arrive by dawn."

"So, we have to keep everyone alive till then."

The Doctor thanked the soldier.

"No. If you use that power anymore, you will definitely die."

"That may be true."

I placed my hand on his chest.

"Don't. I just got you back. I don't want to lose you."

The Doctor embraced me.

"You will never lose me, Exia. I'll be by your side."

I clutched him tightly.

"Let's go."

I held the Doctor's hand tightly. We walked towards the camp. Just as the soldier mentioned, Jessica and the other doctors were swamped. I heard the shouts and groans of the wounded soldiers. The doctors couldn't keep up. The soldiers would start dying soon if this continued.

The Doctor let go of my hand and walked forward. He held out his palm towards the camp. A golden swirl of energy surrounded the Doctor. I tried to get close to him but the energy pushed me back. The golden mass of energy slowly turned into streams and flowed towards the camp. The streams connected with every wounded soldier. After all the wounded were linked, the stream suddenly turned red. It started flowing faster towards the Doctor.

I looked at the Doctor and saw him desperately trying to stand. Blood slowly trickled down from his eyes. The red energy completely swallowed him. After a few seconds, the energy dissipated. The Doctor stood still. He staggered. I caught him before he fell and laid his head on my lap. His skin felt ice cold. He slowly opened his eyes.

"The wounded ..."

"They're fine. Worry about yourself."

"Good."

My tears were falling before I noticed it.

"You're so stubborn."

He raised his hands and wiped my tears.

"I'll be waiting for you."

I held his hand. I felt his pulse slowing down.

"Your smile … Can I see it?"

I thought of everything that happened from when we first met. All the memories. That night at the park. How was I able to smile properly then? I remembered what I thought of. I imagined the Doctor smiling and extending his hand.

"Let's go, Exia."

I smiled. The Doctor clutched my hand tightly.

"Such a pretty smile. As expected of my angel."

He slowly let go of my hand. I cradled his head and didn't move.

A few hours later, at dawn, the war was called off. A treaty was proposed but in essence, we won the war. When the Commander returned, the entire army stood silent before the Doctor. The Commander knelt down.

"You finally got the ending you wanted. I'm proud of you, old friend."

The entire army cheered for the Doctor. The Commander and a few soldiers carried the Doctor and buried him. I stood before his grave. I put my arm around Jessica and consoled her. Her eyes were all red. After a few weeks, the townspeople returned. When they heard the story of the Doctor, the entire town gathered before his grave. Every single person prayed.

Jessica took over his clinic. I felt lost initially but I gathered all my strength and packed my bags. I walked into the Doctor's room and found one of his coats. I picked it up and held it close. I wore it and walked downstairs. Jessica burst into tears when she saw my luggage.

"Take care, Jessica."

"I don't know if I can live up to someone like him."

I leaned against her head.

"You are the one he chose. Be more confident. The Doctor always makes the best choices."

Jessica hugged me tightly.

"Take care, Exia."

"I'll come visit some time."

I walked outside the clinic. The golden portal opened and "he" walked out. "He" grabbed my luggage.

"Shall we go?"

I followed "him" and we ended up at his apartment.

"I told you he was quite an interesting fellow."

"You knew he was going to destroy the power along with himself?"

"Ah, you noticed it? He told me he was going to do that when he was unconscious."

"He would've survived if he hadn't done that. You could've stopped him."

"Even if he had survived, he wouldn't be alive. He would've been stuck in a vegetative state."

"But …"

"Exia, this is what he chose to do. Besides, I couldn't have done anything. His resolve is much greater than any human. His greed, his ambition. They're all too great. That's why he was the only one who was able to survive for so long."

I looked down sadly. "He" came closer and placed his hand on my head.

"It's a good ending, Exia. He died without running away and died in the lap of the woman he loves."

I pushed away my sadness. Why am I sad? He taught me to smile. I won't lose that precious gift.

"The Doctor said he will wait for me. I know he will keep his promise."

I looked up and smiled at him. "He" looked at me surprised.

"I will see him again. I'm sure."

"He" smiled.

....

BLINDFOLD

A man without anything … someone who had lost his family and friends. With nowhere else to go, I sat down in a dark alleyway waiting for death to swiftly take me away. Instead of the darkness and coldness of death, I found a bright light in front of me. It took the shape of a woman. She wore a blue gown that was slightly faded and her shoes were all worn down. But the most intriguing part of her was her face. While she had very fair skin and her face was petite, all my attention was focused on her eyes which was covered by a blindfold made of flowers. She opened her basket and pulled out a big loaf of bread. She knelt down and handed it to me.

"Here you go."

I looked at the bread in her hand.

"It's ok. You can take it."

"How did you know I'm here?"

"Oh, I have keen senses. You still haven't taken it, aren't you hungry?"

"I don't take things from people just like that. After all, nothing in this world is free."

"That is true. Then think of this as a way for me to satisfy myself."

I took the bread from her hands and started to eat it.

"You shouldn't be out here alone. It's dangerous. What if you get preyed upon!"

She laughed.

"Thank you for worrying about me, but I will be fine. After all, it's not like I've lived a rosy life."

Somehow, even though I couldn't see her eyes, I felt a pang of sadness emanate from her.

"What happened to you?"

"My sight? It's just a curse. A rotten curse that cannot be dispelled. Or rather, I've given up on it."

She sighed and turned away.

"It's been a while since someone made me talk so much. Well, it was nice talking to you …"

"Rumi."

She laughed but immediately closed her mouth.

"I'm sorry. You seem like a really big man …"

"Big men can't have that name?"

"No, it's nothing like that. I was just surprised."

She started walking away.

"What's your name?"

She turned around and smiled.

"Eris."

After that, I started walking out of the alleyway in hopes of meeting Eris. I constantly wondered on why I was so eager to meet her. Every step I took was met with the usual disdainful stares of people. But Eris' stare was warm. Even after years of people looking at me like trash, I couldn't get used to it. How did Eris see me?

I finally found her talking to one of the shopkeepers. After she finished talking, she started walking in the other direction. I followed her until I saw a group of men teasing her and trying to touch her.

"Hey, you're looking quite nice. Oh, you're blind? Don't worry, we will take good care of you." They sneered.

The people around slowly distanced themselves out of fear. My heart swelled up and I walked forward with conviction. Before I could do anything, Eris dropped her bag of groceries. She grabbed the closest man's hand and twisted it until a sickening crunch was heard. The man howled in pain. Before the other two could react, she grabbed one of them and threw them onto the ground. The third slowly backed away. She nonchalantly picked up her groceries and resumed walking.

I ended up following her all the way to her house.

When she reached the entrance of her house, she suddenly turned back and faced me.

"Rumi, why are you following me?"

"I'm surprised you could tell it was me."

"There's only one big man who would want to follow me all the way here. If you take a look around, you'll see that I'm not exactly very popular in the town."

"Shouldn't you be more careful?"

"Are you going to hurt me?"

"I want to know more about you, Eris."

She turned around.

"I don't think that's good for either of us. But why don't you come in? I'll prepare a nice warm meal for you."

Eris's cooking was delicious. After we ate, she pulled out a bottle of wine and two glasses.

"So, Rumi, why don't you tell me something about yourself first?"

"What's there to say? I'm just a normal straggler. I had everything before. Now I have nothing."

"Is that really all there is to you?"

I downed my glass of wine in one gulp.

"I used to be good with people. Somehow, travelling from place to place, I lost myself. And by losing myself, I became someone who truly belonged nowhere."

I tried to imagine my family's faces but nothing appeared. Some child I am.

I felt a warm hand on my face.

"Don't say something so sad. You'll find your place. Until that time comes, you can call this home."

"Thank you. Now, what's your story?"

"Oh, its shorter than yours. This is a curse inflicted on me by someone. I guess he might be called god. Every single person I've met always talks about the beauty of this world. It's something that I have been enamoured with since I was able to listen to people. I want to see all the beautiful things in this world."

"Is there any way I can help you?"

"Help? Why?"

"Well, just think of it as a way to satisfy myself."

"There is a way to enable my vision, but …"

"But?"

"No, it's nothing. You shouldn't be involved in this."

I sat closer.

"Tell me."

I saw her slowly weighing the options.

"You have to perform ten labours. I don't know what labours would be given."

"That's all?"

"It's not like they'll be easy. They are given randomly and are to be finished quickly."

"How do I start?"

"You have to drink my blood. But, are you sure? You may lose your life."

"It's not like I have anything to lose."

The bare truth stung me. Eris picked up the knife on the table. She slowly cut her arm. As the blood started flowing down her arm, I held it and drank her blood. My vision instantly began to fade.

I woke up hours later on Eris' lap.

"How long was I out?"

"About five hours."

"So how will I know about the labours?"

"You will get a vision of it. It takes a day for it to start, so shall we do a little shopping before that?"

"Why?"

"Well, somehow, I can't let you do work in tattered rags. Please, I insist."

The next morning, Eris and I went out to the local tailor. Even though she was blind, it looked like her fashion sense was on point. She finished all the preparations. Soon, the outfit was ready. I picked it up and tried it on. As I looked in a mirror, I couldn't recognize the person standing before it. Eris came up to my room.

"Do you like your clothes?"

"It looks great. Thank you, Eris."

She smiled.

"Dinner's ready."

We ate dinner and cleaned up the table. The next morning, I woke up early and found Eris sitting at the table.

"Good morning, Eris."

"Ah, good morning, Rumi. How are you feeling?"

"Zero visions."

"Maybe it'll take some more time."

"You sure this will actually work?"

Eris puffed up her chest.

"You think I'm lying?"

I chuckled nervously. I helped her set the table for lunch. Suddenly, I felt a blinding pain. I dropped a plate. The plate shattered into pieces. A vision immediately formed in my head.

Eris quickly came to my side.

"Rumi? What's wrong?!"

"I just had a vision. I have to go now."

Before I could leave, Eris grabbed my hand.

"Wait, I want you to take this."

She walked into her room and brought out a sword. The sword felt very light and its scabbard was decorated beautifully. I pulled it out and saw my reflection along the blade. A sharp, fine sword.

"I hope you know how to use it."

"I have some idea."

I rushed out of the door towards the location. When I reached there, it looked like everything was orchestrated. The people there were waiting for me. A merchant quickly called for me.

"You're Rumi, right? I'm the merchant who hired you. I look forward to your protection."

Who was this guy? How did he know my name? Was this part of the labour?

I felt a tight grip on my shoulder.

"Rumi? Are you alright?"

I decided to stop questioning it.

"Shall we start?"

I helped the merchant load all the goods into the carriage. Two more-armed people joined us for the ride. As we were travelling to the next town, the labour finally started showing its difficulty. The first obstacle was a group of bandits who ambushed us for money. I pushed the merchant down while the two guards began fighting the enemy. I jumped into the fray as well. After a few minutes, the dust settled and the bandits were defeated. But one of the guards was injured. I bandaged him up as best as I could while the carriage kept moving to its destination. The second obstacle was a muddy road. The two rear wheels got caught in the mud and we were unable to move. To make matters worse, it started raining heavily. I signalled to the healthy guard and the two of us got down from the carriage. We bent down and lifted the carriage up from the mud. The horses were slowly starting to get restless. We found shelter in a nearby cave and decided to stay the night. I checked the bandages of the injured guard and volunteered to keep a lookout. As the three men slept peacefully, I stared up at the angry sky.

"I wonder if Eris has gone to sleep. I hope she isn't too worried about me. As if ..."

I chuckled.

"Maybe I'll ask her to cook plenty of dishes for me when I get back."

After a few days, we reached the town. The merchant finished his business while I helped carry the injured guard to the nearby clinic. We met up at the end of the day and stayed at the local inn. After we finished dinner, the merchant pulled me aside.

"I just wanted to thank you for helping me."

"It's fine. I did it for myself."

The merchant bellowed.

"I see you've grasped the merchants' motto. Anyways, I will pay you back for the help."

"Thank you."

The next morning, as we all started getting into the carriage, I got another vision. My head felt like it was splitting apart.

"Rumi, are you getting in?"

"I'm sorry. You guys carry on. I'll come back later. I have some work to do here."

While the guards looked confused, the merchant looked at me with determination. He grabbed a small pouch and threw it at me.

"There you go. Don't be gone too long. Your wife will worry."

I cracked a smile.

"Tell her I'll be back soon."

The injured guard thanked me sincerely. The merchant waved at me as he left for home.

I started walking to the place I saw in my vision.

ERIS

The first few days without Rumi were fine. But as time progressed, my worries kept piling. Why am I feeling like this? I'm only using him to get my sight. As if I'd care if something happens to him. He could even be dead by now.

Something snapped in me. My heart crawled up my throat. I felt sick. I clutched my mouth and fell to my knees. No, I don't want anything to happen to him. I don't want him to die. I tried to distract myself.

How would he look like? His name sounds beautiful. He also said he's quite big. I smiled a little bit and tried to be oblivious to any grave thoughts.

A few days later, as I was shopping for dinner, I heard the sound of hooves nearing. I heard people call out for the merchant and walked towards the sound. My heart felt light. Rumi was back. I heard the horses stop and the sound of boots jumping onto the ground. I felt a light sensation on my hand.

"Rumi …!"

"I'm sorry to disappoint you."

I realized that I wasn't talking to Rumi.

"Oh, the merchant? I'm sorry. I thought it was Rumi."

I tried to search for his voice but I couldn't.

"If you're looking for Rumi, he isn't here."

I dropped my bag.

"What do you mean?"

He isn't here. Wait, does that mean …? No. I don't want to be responsible for his death. Rumi? Where are you?

I began hyperventilating. The merchant touched my shoulder gently.

"Calm down. He told me he has work to do in the town. He took out several bandits by himself. I'm sure he's fine."

I slowly calmed myself. He'll come back to me. I'm sure. I'll cook plenty of dishes for him when he comes back. He loves to eat.

RUMI

I lost track of the number of days and the number of labours. Each labour went on for several days and there was no prior confirmation of when each one would end. All I could do was hope to finish each one and wait for the next vision. After a while, the visions stopped. I decided to stay a few more days before leaving. I started back on my way home. I gripped my sword tightly, thinking of Eris.

I finally reached home. I felt exhausted. I knocked at Eris' door and heard loud footsteps. As she opened the door, I felt a little of my exhaustion disappear. She wore a green gown this time.

"I'm home, Eris."

"Rumi!"

She hugged me tightly.

"Welcome home!"

I sat down at the table as she brought me some freshly prepared, steaming hot dishes.

"How long have I been gone?"

"Almost a month. Do you know how many labours you finished?"

"I'm sorry. I couldn't keep track of them."

"It's fine. You're home now. Eat up, I prepared plenty of dishes."

As soon as I ate her food, I gagged. The food tasted like dirt. I picked up the glass of wine and drank. I tried my best not to spit it out.

What is happening? Eris's cooking is delicious. Why does it taste like this?

I kept my reactions to a minimum to prevent Eris from noticing. I gulped down everything so that Eris wouldn't worry about me. Dinner was the same tasteless affair. I ended up feeling even more exhausted.

I got a vision late at midnight. I opened the door as quietly as I could and left the house. Luckily, I was done by morning. I slowly walked through the door just to see Eris come downstairs.

"Good morning, Eris."

"Good morning. I'm about to start breakfast. Why don't you come help me?"

I smiled and joined her in the kitchen. The food still tasted horrible to me. Suddenly, Eris got up and walked towards me.

"Eris? What's wrong?"

"How was today's food, Rumi?"

"How? Maybe you could've lessened the spice a little bit."

Eris bent down and touched my face.

"I didn't put anything spicy in it, Rumi."

I bit my tongue.

"Why didn't you tell me before?"

"How did you know?"

"You think just because I'm blind, you can hide everything from me? I know how you eat when you eat something delicious. I can feel the happiness from the other room. All I feel now is graveness."

"I just didn't want you to worry."

Eris crossed her arms.

"I will always worry about you. You finished another labour before breakfast, didn't you?"

I looked down at my plate.

"There's no way you could wake up before me."

"How does it matter? The sooner I finish it, the sooner you can start seeing the world."

"And you don't care what happens to you?"

I got up and banged the table. I couldn't seem to put my feelings across to her.

"It doesn't matter! It's not like I have anything to live for. If I die in the process of helping you, then it's fine."

Eris rushed towards me and slapped me hard. The pain pulsed through my body.

"At first, I wanted to just use you and make you complete the labours so that I would be able to see. But when you started working so hard for me, I just couldn't think like that anymore. I started missing you, I wanted you to stay at home with me. I don't want to see anything if I'm going to lose you!" Her voice turned hoarse with pain. She broke down in tears.

Eris stormed out of the house. I sank back into my chair. What did I just say to her? I wanted to come home as well. I wanted to be with her as well. I should've told her all of that. I shouldn't have let her be mad at me. I'll tell her everything right now.

Just then, I got a blinding vision. This vision hurt more than any of the other visions. I fell from the chair and couldn't get up. After a few minutes, it ended. I got up to my knees and took a deep breath.

"This must be the final labour."

I'll tell everything to Eris once I'm done with it. I finished my breakfast and left a note on the table.

ERIS

After I stormed off, I kept walking around town until I heard my name called. I recognized the merchant's voice.

"Eris, how have you been?"

"I've been better."

"Ah, did you fight with Rumi?"

"Is it that obvious?"

"A little bit. Why don't you talk to me about it?"

The merchant and I walked into the storehouse and sat down. I explained everything. The merchant listened patiently and then chuckled.

"That does sound like Rumi."

"What do I do?"

"You're scared, aren't you? Scared of him not returning?"

"Terribly scared."

"Then just go and tell him. If there's one thing I know about that man, it's that he cherishes you. On that trip, he would look at his sword fondly. One night, when he volunteered to be a lookout, I heard him mutter your name. Smiled like an idiot as well. Only thing you two need is a proper talk."

He helped me up.

"The two of you are so young. Don't waste your time apart like this."

"But I slapped him. How can I face him again?"

The merchant laughed loudly.

"It is just a slap. It probably woke him up."

He grabbed my hand.

"Ok. I'll come with you. Let's go."

"Thank you."

The two of us walked back home. I opened the door and called out for Rumi. I didn't hear an answer. The merchant walked over to the table.

"There's a note here. Probably from Rumi."

"Can you read it out for me?"

"I have one last job to do. I'll settle everything and come home."

Rumi …

The merchant sighed.

"Ah, I came here for nothing. Eris, looks like your problem is almost solved. I'll take my leave then."

"Thank you again."

The merchant left. I closed the door and picked up the note. I held it close to my heart.

"I'm waiting, Rumi."

I waited for several days. This wasn't very different from the first labour. He was gone for weeks then. I can wait some more time. This mental strength gradually dwindled with each passing day. Waiting for him to come home started getting agonizing. How did my daily routine change so much? My mind was stuck on Rumi. It felt like a void in my heart.

Finally, one day, I heard a knock on my door. I rushed to the door and opened it.

"Sorry, Eris. It's just me."

I welcomed the merchant in but was crestfallen inside.

"Have you heard anything about Rumi?"

"No, I haven't. It looks like he isn't in any of the neighbouring towns."

The merchant's answer only added to my grief.

I could feel my anguish suffocating me.

"He'll be fine, Eris." He tried to reassure. But in vain.

The merchant and I chatted some more before he left. That night, I wasn't able to sleep. Around dawn, I heard something bang against the door. I cautiously walked towards the door and opened it. I heard a body fall on the floor.

"Rumi!" I gasped.

I knelt down and touched the face. I heard him mutter something weakly. I pressed my ear closer.

"Eris …"

I recognized the voice that called my name so lovingly.

"Rumi!"

I hugged him tightly.

"I'm here for you."

He slowly got up and turned to face me. He touched my face gently.

"Eris."

He touched my blindfold and pulled it off. I felt light flood into my eyes. It took me a few minutes to adjust to everything. As soon as I was able to focus, I saw Rumi's face clearly. I was drawn to his face. It was beautifully shaped. His pale skin almost glowed. I touched his face.

"You're beautiful."

"That was my line."

He stared deep into my eyes.

"I'm home, Eris."

I felt a tear roll down my eye. I smiled.

"Welcome home, Rumi."

Rumi spent a week recovering gradually. That day he called out to me from downstairs. I quickly finished packing and stood in front of the mirror. I looked closer and inspected my face. No matter how many times I saw myself, I couldn't get used to it. I walked around town the entire week, taking in everyone's faces. The merchant almost fainted when he saw me without the blindfold. Everyone in the town was equally surprised.

I quickly walked downstairs to see Rumi holding a huge bag.

"Are you sure you should be getting ready to travel?"

Rumi laughed.

"I could travel the entire world and still be fine. Besides, you'll nurse me back if I fall sick, right?"

He reached his hand out.

"Let's go explore this beautiful world, Eris."

"Together."

I grabbed his hand and we both walked out into the light that embraced us lovingly.

....

SIGNAL

For a long, long time, I would always be standing in front of a signal. The signal was always red. As I kept waiting for it to turn green, everything around me would continue moving. I was always trapped by this signal. I would constantly get transported to this place whenever I looked at Haru. Just like his name, his gentle brightness and warmth would permeate his surroundings. Most of the time, I would be blinded by him. I don't remember when we got close but we would always end up walking home together. I remember the first time he walked up to me to ask me back when we were sophomores.

"Hey, can we walk home together?"

I looked around him to see if someone had given him some kind of dare or challenge. After all, we only spoke a few times out of necessity. He grabbed my face and redirected my focus back to him.

"I'm asking you because I want to. Can I walk you home?"

"Sure."

He let go of my face and turned around quickly. I saw his hands shake with excitement. He turned around and gave me a huge smile. That sight of his smile seemed to have got permanently etched into my mind. That was the moment I fell in love with him. Soon, walking home with him became a ritual I waited for. I was able to spend a lot of time with the person I love. Can I be this happy?

We would stop by a convenience store every now and then while going home. He would always drink black coffee while I drank milk. One time, out of curiosity, I grabbed his hand and sipped a bit of his coffee. He looked at me surprised. As soon as I swallowed it, I realized my mistake and began coughing. Haru laughed out loudly.

"Serves you right. Why did you have to drink mine!" He teased.

Immediately after, he suddenly pulled my hand close and took a sip of my coffee.

He raised his cup and gestured with the same teasing smile, "Somehow, this tastes extra delicious now."

I looked down at my can and blushed, the same thought was hovering in my mind too. He got up and waved at me.

"Let's go home."

Those twenty minutes of happiness after school continued on without any interruption. My feelings for him grew stronger with each passing day. One day, I made up my mind. I gathered my resolve and set out to confess to him. As I walked around school trying to find Haru, I finally spotted him around the corner. As I neared him, I saw a girl talking to him quietly. It looked like she was confessing her feelings to him. He bowed down slightly. I felt relief wash over me.

When I was transported in front of the signal, it finally turned green. As I lifted my foot to walk forward, I suddenly heard something.

"I'm in love with someone else."

The signal suddenly turned red. My foot came down and I was still standing in the same place. My resolve crumbled. I was stuck before that red signal.

When Haru later found me and we started walking home, I stayed silent. Haru knew that something was wrong. Halfway, he stopped me.

"Come this way. I have something to show you."

He led me to a long spiralling road going uphill. Once we reached the top, we looked out over the city. He opened his bag and pulled out a piece of paper. He wrote something on it and folded it into a plane.

"I used to come here a lot whenever I was troubled by something. I would write down what I wanted to do most and then throw it off. Somehow, as I saw the plane fly in the distance, I would gain the courage to do it."

He walked towards the edge and threw the plane. It flew across the red sky towards the sun. It was a beautiful sight. I ended up smiling without realizing.

Haru looked at me and smiled. He murmured to himself.

"So, my plane routine worked again. Truly, a miracle."

I grabbed a piece of paper and wrote down my desire inside it. "Confess to Haru." As I threw it, the courage flowed into me. I clenched my fist tightly. I turned around to face Haru.

"Haru, there's something very important I want to tell you tomorrow. Can you meet me here?"

He looked at me surprised, his eyes twinkling.

"Sure. Then, you leave early. I'll finish off my work and come as quickly as I can."

I smiled widely.

The next day, after school, I rushed up the road towards the meeting spot. I stood there, collecting all my emotions and making sure I was able to say it. Time passed and Haru was nowhere to be seen. I ended up waiting until the moon started to rise. I started walking back down the road dejected. What happened? Haru isn't the type to ditch me.

Suddenly, I heard a bunch of people chatting. I looked down at the road and saw a lot of blood. An accident? As I heard more and more details of the people speaking, a fear began to grow in my heart. Finally, I overheard one of the bystanders speak.

"It is so sad to see such a young boy suffer an accident like this. His uniform was also from the nearby school."

I immediately ran up to the woman.

"I'm sorry! Can you please tell me which hospital he is in?"

I started running as hard as I could to the hospital. My lungs were nearly bursting but I didn't dare stop. No. Haru, don't go! Please … let it not be Haru. When I reached the hospital, I asked the receptionist about the student who was admitted recently. She referred me to one of the rooms. I ran up the stairs. Finally, I found a woman with her face in her palms sitting on one of the chairs. I instantly recognized her.

"No. No. Please no."

The doctor came outside and sat down next to the woman. He shook his head and clutched the woman's hands. The woman broke down into tears. I fell down to my knees. Tears poured down my face.

Why? Why did it have to happen? I didn't get a chance to tell him. I loved him. I never got to say I loved him. I never got to go on a date with him.

The signal turned off. I was permanently stuck in place. A week later, a funeral for Haru was held in school. The entire school was sombre and dull. Without Haru, the school had lost all its brightness for me. I became a senior and mindlessly prepared for my exams. The entire school had moved on but I couldn't. I kept thinking of Haru at all times. I could see his smiling face constantly. Even during the final exams, I could only picture Haru's face. If I had confessed, what would have been his answer?

As I walked back home alone, I suddenly saw someone calling for me. I looked up and saw that it was Haru's mother.

"Hello, dear. I haven't seen you since the funeral. How were your exams?"

"They were fine, Aunty."

"Do you have any plans after school?"

"I haven't planned anything yet, Aunty. I might go for a local university."

"I see. Well, why don't you come inside? I'll pour you a nice cup of coffee."

"It's ok, Aunty. I don't want to impose on you."

"No, I insist."

She grabbed my hand and pulled me inside.

"Feel free to sit anywhere you like."

Aunty walked into the kitchen while I looked around in the hall. This was my first time in Haru's house. Behind me was a picture of Haru with some incense burning before it. That smile of his that used to erase any worry of mine now seemed as if it was a burden.

Aunty placed a hot cup of coffee on the table. I looked at it surprised.

"You like it with lots of milk, don't you? Haru used to tell me that."

"He used to talk about me?"

"All the time. I was surprised you didn't introduce yourself to me directly."

"Sorry, I was …"

I was what? There was no excuse. I could've come here sooner. But I wasn't ready to.

"I understand, dear. You loved him a lot, didn't you?"

"How did you–"

"I saw it. You were grieving just as much as me. I know you loved him with all your heart."

"I did. But I never got an answer from him. I was afraid to tell him sooner. Afraid of being rejected. I held it all in. By the time I was ready, I had already lost him."

I felt a lump in my throat. As I looked at my own reflection in the mug, I felt disgusted. The coffee tasted bitter. Suddenly, Aunty got up.

"Come with me."

I got up and followed her. She stopped before a room.

"This is Haru's room. The last time I entered it was the morning he died. When he found me there, he told me to quickly get out. He blushed fiercely and told me that there was something very special in the room and only that person had to see it. It's not that hard to guess who that person was. Now, I can finish this job."

She opened the door and I walked inside. I gasped loudly. The entire room was filled with paper airplanes hanging from the ceiling.

"I was always curious on what he wanted to do. His habit of writing his biggest desire is something I also follow every now and then."

I plucked the nearest airplane and opened it.

"I want to confess to Aki tomorrow."

I refused to believe it at first, I went and plucked the next one. The same thing was written in it. Another, another. I plucked all the planes and found the same thing written on it. I slumped against the wall. Tears fell down on the paper.

He loved me. He was in love with me. I … I didn't have to worry about being rejected. I should've … I should've …

I gasped for breath. I sobbed loudly. I felt Aunty wrap her arms around me.

As I was transported back in front of the signal, it suddenly turned back on. That red light that was constantly on … I realized that I could've crossed it any time I wanted.

I grabbed a piece of paper from Haru's desk and wrote on it. I walked up the road towards that very spot. I threw it off the edge.

The very instant the airplane started flying I saw all of Haru's airplanes fly beside it. The signal in front of me turned green and I walked forward. I kept walking forward until the signal was no more.

On that airplane slowly flying towards the setting sun was written,

"I want to run forward without any fear with all my might."

WORDS

My happiest memories always revolved around artwork. It was mainly my Dad who cultivated those memories. He would always have me sit on a really high stool and paint on his canvas. Sometimes, he would let me paint over some important paintings and then praise me. My Mom would come into the studio and scold Dad severely before pulling me away. Dad would laugh it off and then start looking at the painting. He kept my scribbling in the painting and would somehow make it even more beautiful. But these paintings would often break the deadline which led his manager, Mom, to scold him further. I grew up in awe of his paintings.

When I reached junior high, I immediately enrolled in the Art Club. I encountered several different people there which broadened my perspectives. I used to come home every day with a new idea in mind. My hands would start itching for a paintbrush the moment I entered Dad's studio. Once I got serious in junior high, Mom ended up splitting the studio into two halves to accommodate me as well. I ended up bringing lots of accolades to my junior high school. Every time I ended up in the staff room to talk to the club advisor, I kept hearing about someone who was bringing fame to the school's literary club. My name and the name "Emily" would keep floating around the staff room after every competition.

Once I graduated junior high, Mom and Dad ended up landing a big job. They started working with a big, reputed gallery which made them even more busy. Most of the days were spent alone with my paintings.

I chose a high school which was close and had a thriving extracurricular environment. The entrance ceremony and everything quickly flashed by. I ignore everything and focused on the Art Club. Finally, club inductions started. The entire campus was in a frenzy as people crowded over the freshman. I pushed my way through the crowd and climbed up to the second floor. I stopped before the sign that said Art Club. I opened the door and saw a group of people talking. They all stopped talking and immediately looked at me. A tall, spectacled guy walked towards me.

"Welcome to the Art Club. I'm the President of the Art Club."

I ignored him and walked towards the paintings. The President raised his eyebrows and stood at the doorway.

"Prez, which painting is yours?"

He came closer and pointed to his painting. I examined the painting closer and pulled out a notepad. I started noting down the possible techniques he could have used. The President looked over my shoulder and grinned.

"If you want to know my techniques, I'll need the sign-up form."

I quickly pulled it out of my bag and handed it to him.

"I look forward to working with all of you."

The entire room laughed at my eagerness and they joined me. I ended up asking all of them questions until the time the school closed. When I reached home, Mom and Dad were busy working in the studio. I walked upstairs to my room and pulled out the notepad. I quickly read all the notes I took and smiled.

"I found a great place."

I ended up looking forward to club activities every single day. The President was a very talented artist. I adored all of his paintings. I could tell that everyone in the Art Club truly cherished the art of painting. Prez would often keep going next door to the Literature Club. One day he called me with him. The Literature Club Room was just as energizing as the Art Club. There were stacks and stacks of books. There were students at the table reading quietly. It felt quite calm and serene. I could tell that the Literature Club and the Art Club were very close when I saw the Literature Club president. She had long black hair and her eyes were sparkling. In front of her were several sheets with text all over them. She got up and walked towards us.

"Leah, I'm here to introduce you to our talented freshman."

He held my shoulder and urged me forward. Leah laughed.

"He seems quite serious."

"He basically ignored me and went straight for the paintings in our very first meeting."

Leah doubled over laughing. I tugged on Prez's sleeve.

"Prez, can you stop bringing that up? I said I'm sorry."

He chuckled and introduced me.

"This is the Literature Club president, Leah. Well, Leah is her pen name but she prefers it over her real name."

I shook her hand.

"Nice to meet you."

"Nice to meet you, too!"

She quickly turned to Prez.

"I forgot. I've got quite an amazing freshman as well."

She turned around and called out to a girl who was sitting at the far end of the table. She had bright blonde hair.

"Emily! Come over here for a second."

The girl slowly walked over. She had beautiful green eyes that mesmerized me.

"This is Emily. She's a great writer."

Emily looked up at me.

"Nice to meet you."

I got caught up looking at her eyes and didn't respond. Prez nudged me. I came back to the real-time scenario.

"Nice to meet you, Emily."

Leah pulled both of us together.

"Now, the two of you have to get along well. See, the Art Club and the Literature Club have a lot of history together. A very tight knit one. And besides, the two of you are in the same class, aren't you?"

Emily and I both looked at each other surprised. Leah and Prez laughed. Leah laughed until she got her eyes teary.

"We're both blessed with a bunch of airheads. It's going to be a great ride."

That night, I somehow slept much better than I had before. The next few months, I frequented the Literature Club and got along well with everyone there. The only person with whom I didn't get along well was Emily. She was always either writing or reading when I visited the club. In class, however, she seemed to be a different person. She was very sociable and always had people around her, talking, discussing and smiling. Somehow it felt like her behaviour in the club room was more real than her mannerisms in class. After months of trying, I finally found my chance one day to connect with her.

She was hunched over what looked like a manuscript. The club room was empty except for the two of us. I sat opposite her and tried to initiate a conversation. But I couldn't find the right timing for it. I ended up sitting there quietly for a while trying to talk to her. She gave a long sigh.

"Stuck in your manuscript?"

I bit my tongue lightly as she stared at me blankly.

"You are the Art Club freshman?"

I felt a mixed sense of happiness and sadness. Happiness arose partly from the fact that at least she remembered this much about me and sadness because I was a still a non-entity to her soul.

"Yes. Is there anything I can help you with?"

"It's not like you can help me but no harm in letting you know that I'm stuck at a certain point in this story. I'm unable to visualize the context so I just can't proceed with my story."

Ah! I saw a path of light illuminate the table leading from me to her. Figuratively, of course. But I felt a sudden sense of happiness that I might be able to help her in some way.

"Can I see that? I think I can help you."

She looked at me sceptically.

"I don't plan on showing this to anyone yet."

"Just a peek won't hurt."

She relented and handed me the manuscript. I read it and was quite impressed. She was a good writer. I could feel the emotions of the characters vividly. After I finished reading the writeup, I pulled out my sketchbook and began drawing the scene where she was stuck.

I drew it and then roughly coloured it. After a few minutes, I put down my pencil and held it out to her.

"It might not help you at all but I had to draw this after reading your story."

I couldn't see her reaction to my drawing. Her face was lowered as she stared intently at the drawing. Suddenly, she grabbed the book from me and held it close.

"You drew this in such a short span of time?" There was sheer astonishment in her expression and I loved it.

"I mean, it's quite shabby and unrefined" I stammered. "But I don't think I left any emotion out of it."

She caressed the drawing absent-mindedly with her long, shapely fingers. My eyes were rivetted at the beauty of her artistic fingers.

"It's beautiful." She said in a somewhat languishing tone. As if her heart was pining for something unfathomable.

I felt a strange kind of acceptance and happiness. I had never felt this way before, I realized. So many people had told me how beautiful and stunning my works were. But somehow when she said it, it felt warmer than any other compliment. I snapped back to reality. When I looked at Emily again, she was staring at me with those big defiant flashing deep green eyes of hers.

"Is there something wrong?"

"Your drawing … 'she muttered'… your drawing is off in a lot of places."

She took out her pen and started writing notes on my drawings. She began pointing out several shortcomings.

"But you just complimented it." I blurted out. I was aghast. How could a person change poles so fast?

"I did but it's far from being a perfect work."

Her expression barely changed as she looked me in the eye.

I gritted my teeth and picked up her manuscript. I started pointed out all the improvement points I could find in her writing as well. She looked at me in disbelief and snatched the manuscript back from me.

"Ah, you're right."

Her disbelief immediately disappeared as she began revising her work.

I picked up my sketchbook and looked at my drawing closely. I strangely realized that all her criticisms weren't absolutely unwarranted. The two of us sat looking at each other. Suddenly, we burst out in laughter. I couldn't really remember what made me laugh. We spent the rest of the day reworking on our creativity based on our mutual suggestions. Somehow, I ended up having much more fun drawing that I ever had. When we were almost done and decided to leave, I saw Prez and Leah smiling widely at the two of us. I blushed fiercely and walked out of the clubroom hurriedly.

Emily and I started meeting regularly after school. We spent hours and hours discussing our works. During finals, we ended up studying together in the Literature Club Room. Soon, the second-year entrance ceremony started. The first club meeting for the year was quite different. The entire Art Club had assembled in the Literature Club Room.

I sat next to Emily as we all wondered why we were gathered here. The room became silent as Leah and Prez entered the room. Leah spoke excitedly.

"Guys, I have some great news! The Literature Club is bringing back the traditional anthology."

She raised her hands above her head and cheered loudly. When she realized that no one else joined her, she looked at Prez dubiously. Prez immediately cheered timidly.

"The Literature Club anthology has always been the club's defining activity but we couldn't end up making it last year. Now that we have fresh members, we can bring it back. This time, let's make it the best anthology this club has ever seen!"

This time the entire room cheered loudly. After the cheering settled, one of the members stood up and asked a question.

"Where does the Art Club fit in here?"

Leah grinned and put her arm around Prez.

"The Art Club is in charge of making the cover. So, they'll have to get acquainted with every member of the Literature Club and have to be involved in the entire process. We can't ask them for anything else since they'll be busy supporting every single club in the school."

Leah announced a few more things before she ended the meeting. Prez and Leah sat down beside me.

"Prez, have you done this before?"

"This is more like a farewell ceremony for the third-year students. After the cultural festival, there aren't any more big events for the Art Club. So, in my first year, while I wanted to be involved in a lot of important club engagements, I held back and let the third years have the most fun."

I grabbed Prez's hand tightly.

"Farewell? I have so much to learn from you. You're leaving?"

Prez patted my head gently.

"Ah, don't worry. I'll still be here for a while. Even Leah."

He looked at her pleading to help him. Leah came and patted my head as well.

"It'll be fine. Why don't you enjoy as much as you can with us now?"

I stood up and slammed the table.

"I'll make this the best festival the two of you have ever seen!"

I grabbed Emily and ran out of the clubroom. Emily didn't seem to notice that I was pulling her.

Leah sat down next to Prez and held his hand tightly.

"We really did get some great members."

She leaned against his shoulder.

Even with the festival two months away, the entire school seemed energized. During the festival month, the preparations began in earnest. As the festival drew closer, classes were grossly neglected with everyone's attention on the festival. The Art Club had mobilized and was everywhere around the campus. Since there were tonnes of banners and signs that had to be made, I barely saw Emily during that time. I knew she would be busy with her contribution to the anthology as well. I kept on working and helping all the other clubs set up. After a week of working, I got a little breathing space. I walked into the Literature Club Room and saw Leah and Prez sitting together. Prez got up when I entered the room

"Welcome back. How's all the work going?"

"It's all progressing well. I just checked up on all the members and they're doing fine as well."

"I feel bad. This is all my job. Maybe I should go check everything."

I walked towards Prez and shoved him down on the seat.

"You focus on the cover of the anthology."

I bent down and stared into his eyes.

"Unless you've already finished it?"

Prez looked down and shook his head.

"That's what I thought."

I walked to the doorway and turned around.

"Prez, make sure you enjoy everything to the maximum."

I smiled and closed the door. The routine continued the next day as I helped out different clubs. Finally, the day before the festival, everything was prepared. Leah and Prez called for a meeting in the Literature Club Room.

"Good work, everyone. We have completed everything and are ready to go."

Emily quickly walked into the room and sat beside me. She looked extremely tired. Everyone focused on Leah hoping that she would unveil the first copy of the anthology. Leah reached out under the desk as everyone held their breath. She smirked and showed us her empty hands.

"All of you are just going to have to wait tomorrow to see it!"

She laughed loudly as everyone groaned in the room.

"Hey, come on guys. This is something very special to me and Prez. So basically, that's all I had to say. All of you can go home now. Bye!"

Everyone sighed and left the club room. Emily and I approached Leah and Prez.

"That was quite brutal, Leah."

She winked at me.

"It's fine. Would you like to have a sneak peek of it?"

I shook my head.

"It's unfair if I see it alone. Besides, I can already tell it'll be great. The two of you did work on it."

Emily grabbed my collar.

"Sorry, the three of you."

The three of them laughed. Prez tapped my shoulder.

"Next year, it'll be your turn."

"A year without Prez? A club without him?"

I slowly began to shut down. Prez grabbed my shoulders.

"I was kidding. I'm still here!"

The four of us walked home together. The three-day big cultural festival was set to begin. The day of the cultural festival, I ended up waking extra early. We would give out our anthologies on the third day so the first two days were mostly free for the two clubs. The Art Club still had to stay a little vigilant in case anyone needed any help at the day. Even with that, Emily and I stayed together. Emily kept wanting to meet up with Leah but I dragged her towards a different direction each time. I realized at the end of the day that I had been holding her hand all this while without realizing. Emily seemed unfazed by it.

"Why did you keep me away from Leah and Prez?"

I scratched my head.

"I wanted them to have some time together. It's their final year after all."

I started murmuring.

"Besides, I wanted to spend time with you alone away from club activities."

Emily came closer.

"Did you say something?"

I realized I said it out loud and quickly turned away.

"Shall we go home?"

The second day of the cultural festival quickly breezed past us. This time, Leah and Prez were with us throughout the day. We had a lot of fun going through the festival, eating lots of food, watching plays and just strolling around school. We stayed back after the second day ended to do some final preparations for the anthologies. The day the two clubs had been waiting for finally arrived. The third day, the festival was open to the public which made the bustling campus even more frenzied. I ended up oversleeping. Dad was beside me trying to wake up.

"Hey! Your cultural festival is today, right?!"

I jumped up out of bed and started getting ready. Dad spoke loudly from downstairs.

"Your mom and I will be visiting your club today! I can't wait to see some fresh youthful artwork!"

I heard Mom reply to him sternly.

"If you finish your work before that!"

I finished getting ready and ran down the stairs.

"I'm leaving, Mom and Dad."

I hurried to school. I reached school and quickly ran to the Literature Club Room where I saw a steady stream of students and attendees pouring inside. I entered the room and found the club members slightly overwhelmed with the volume of responsibilities. I dropped my bag in the locker and chipped in to help them out with the rush. Once the crowd thinned, I turned to Leah and Prez.

"I'm so sorry. I ended up oversleeping."

Leah chuckled.

"It's fine. You're not the only one who overslept today."

She turned around and pointed at Emily. Emily's eyes were baggy and she had dark circles under her eyes. I smiled seeing Emily struggling not to fall asleep. My smile paused halfway as I remembered something.

"Prez! The anthology, I didn't get a chance to see it!"

Prez smiled and handed it to me.

"I knew you'd say that, so I picked out a copy for you."

I looked at the anthology cover and gasped. It was very beautiful. The cover had a girl who was rearranging the stars at night. The cover just felt like Prez.

"It's amazing, Prez."

Prez blushed and combed his fingers carelessly through his thick hair.

"Oh, it's nothing. Try reading it. You'll fall in love with the anthology."

I opened it and started reading it. Once I started, I just did not have the mind to put it down. I settled comfortably in a corner and continued. I could feel the others around me pottering about doing nothing or just engaged in chit chats. I was oblivious to the happenings around.

The stories were short ones. I enjoyed every single one. Leah's story was quite engaging and liked it. But somehow Emily's story resonated more with me. I could connect more with her writing. Once I finished off and put the anthology down, I found Prez looking at me curiously.

"Well, what do you think?"

"It's a great collective effort, Leah. Your story was really good."

As soon as I said that, my eyes drifted towards Emily. I was still trying to decipher the feeling I experienced while I read her story. It felt as if I could see everything through her eyes. I loved every second of it. It made me feel so connected to her.

Leah and Prez smirked at me. A loud voice at the door interrupted my thoughts. I recognized that voice instantly.

"Oh! This is a high school! Oh, my son! Dear, I've found the boy!"

Everyone in the room immediately went silent. I felt all of their eyes on me. I turned around slowly.

"Dad, calm down." I quickly adjusted his blazer.

He quickly changed his demeanour and straightened his tie, trying to look composed. He coughed and spoke in a seemingly dignified tone, which I knew was not his nature.

"I apologize for the loud noise, everyone."

He walked towards the table in a dignified manner and picked up a copy of the anthology. He immediately resumed his loud and boisterous demeanour.

"Whoa! This artwork is magnificent. These techniques with these colours! I can actually feel the emotion! Where is the artist who did this?"

Prez slowly raised his hand. Dad immediately ran towards him and grabbed his shoulder tightly.

"My boy, this is quite good! I can see lots of potential in you."

Dad quickly skimmed through the entire anthology. He turned to Leah.

"And you wrote this first story, right? What a great couple, I must say! The two of you are the definition of youth! A match made in heaven! Please invite me to your wedd ..." His elation was half-complete. His unfinished sentence hung mid-air as a powerful presence entered the classroom.

Dad quickly perked up. Mom came up and touched his shoulder lightly. Dad's face went pale and he apologized quickly. She quickly apologized to Leah and Prez.

"I'm sorry about that. He always becomes overemotional when he sees good artwork."

She whispered in Prez's ear.

"He doesn't give out compliments easily though."

I saw an unadulterated joy on Prez's face. Mom picked up a copy of the anthology as well. She sat down and started reading it. Mom's reading habit was outrageous. If something piqued her interest, she would forget everything else in her life and get sucked into the book. Thinking the same would happen to this anthology, I chuckled.

Some more time elapsed, while everyone had resumed their normal chatter, Mom continued her reading voraciously.

At last, she put it down, "This is quite a great read."

She turned around to face all the students.

"Good work on this, everyone. I enjoyed it thoroughly."

After the brief but unnecessary fiasco, she dragged Dad out with her. Somehow with their exit, the club room's atmosphere was better than it could have ever been. After a few more hours, the festival finally ended. We had a small party in the club room. Time flew by and it was time to stage our next event. The third years' graduation. After the ceremony was over, everyone met up outside on the courtyard instead of the usual club room. Somehow, even though Leah and Prez talked and acted in the same familiar fashion, I felt as if the distance between us has increased somewhat. It made me incredibly sad. My mind strayed in the midst of sad thoughts. I heard people clap for something. Then people started clapping again. I couldn't focus in any of those. All I could focus was on the fact that I shall not see these two at school anymore. I felt someone's hand on my shoulder. I refocused and saw Prez smile at me gently.

"Once again, here is your new Art Club President."

He turned me around to the crowd. Everyone cheered for me. I looked back at Prez.

"Huh? What are you saying, Prez? I'm the President?"

"I have no doubt in my mind. You'll make a fine president."

"But …"

"This isn't goodbye, you know. Leah and I both will always be just a call away."

I hugged Prez tightly.

"I'm going to miss you, Prez!"

"I'll miss you too."

After a long hug, I felt confident I wouldn't cry. I looked at Prez and Leah in their uniforms one last time to make sure it was ingrained in my memory.

"Prez, if you end up marrying her, you better invite me."

"Ah, don't go saying stuff like that!"

Leah stepped in between us.

"Why shouldn't he say stuff like that?"

Prez blushed lightly.

"It's embarrassing."

Suddenly, Emily stepped in front of me.

"You two are dating?"

The three of us stared at her dumbfoundedly. I grabbed her arm.

"You didn't know that?"

She shook her head.

"They didn't even try to hide it. Everyone in the school pretty much knows."

"Congratulations on dating each other."

The three of us laughed harder than we ever did together.

Nothing eventful happened during the session break. Leah and Prez ended up getting admitted to the same university. They both started packing up their things to move. Emily and I helped them pack. After we said our goodbyes, I lost track of time. The entrance ceremony began again. Hearing it for the third time felt very different. New faces, new environment, a new year. Emily and I were in our third year now. I realized that we've been together for quite some time now. I can't remember a school memory where I wasn't with her. After the first day ended, even though the club hadn't started yet, I got the keys from the advisor. I stood before the closed club room door silently. I knew that when I would open the door, I wouldn't find the same smiling people I loved inside. I opened the Art Club room and stepped inside. This place that was filled with such happy memories, now seemed desolate and empty. Almost as if all the colour that was present in this room was non-existent. I suddenly felt a warm sensation around my back. I looked behind and saw Emily hug me from behind.

"Emily …"

"You don't have to act so strong all the time. I know how you feel."

I held her hands.

"I'm fine now. Thank you."

Slowly, the Art Club room began taking on a different, bright colour.

Once clubs began activity, Emily and I were quite busy as club presidents with our own work. But even after we finished all our work with our clubs, we would sit together. I wondered if this is how Prez and Leah felt. At the end of each day, were these moments their happiest? I decided to stop thinking about them and focused on the girl sitting next to me. She always looked so serious reading. Her face would change every time she encountered a twist in the story or she would smile lightly when she read about something happy. I always ended up losing my track of time when I saw her read. Once she finished reading, the two of us locked the club rooms and went home. That day, it started raining suddenly. Fortunately, we were right outside my house. I pulled her into the shade.

"You can stay inside till the rain stops."

I rang the bell and I heard Dad's hurried footsteps. He was already carrying a towel with him.

"Here you go, son."

He looked at Emily and froze for a second. He then ran back into the house and brought another towel.

"Here you go."

Emily took the towel and the two of us entered. We dried ourselves and walked inside. Dad peeked at us from around the corner while Mom approached us.

"Ah, you were part of the Literature Club, weren't you? I remember seeing you at the festival."

"Nice to meet you, Ma'am. I'm Emily. I'm a friend of your son's."

"No need to be so formal with us. Anyways, Emily. I remember your story. It was very well written."

Emily smiled while Dad nodded from behind her.

"Why don't you go take a bath now, dear? I'll leave some spare clothes for you and I'll wash your uniform."

"Thank you, Aunty."

Emily walked into the bathroom and Mom went upstairs to get her some clothes. Dad quickly pulled me into the living room.

"Who is she? Your girlfriend?"

I muffled my Dad's voice with the palm of my hand.

"You remember that story you said you liked a lot from last year's anthology?"

Dad nodded.

"That was her story."

Dad put his arm around me.

"My son is growing up so quickly. I'm so proud."

After Emily came out, I quickly took a bath as well. Emily sat down in my room.

"Can I take a look around your room?"

"Sure."

I quickly made sure there wasn't anything embarrassing in my room. She picked up some of my drawings and looked at them.

"These are nice drawings."

I waited to hear her criticisms as an afterthought but she didn't tell any of them. She looked at my face and understood what I was thinking.

"I become like that when my writing is involved. Otherwise, I don't analyse people's works. I like all of your work. They make me feel warm. I could look at them forever and not be bored."

"Then you can keep looking at them. I'll draw as many as you want."

She looked at me confused.

"What are you saying?"

"I'll draw for you from now on. I'll dedicate everything I have to you."

The realization dawned upon her. I saw her slightly blush.

"I won't accept something simple like this. Bring me everything you have."

I chuckled and got up.

"This cultural festival, I'll give you everything I have."

The rain cleared up. Emily prepared to leave. Before she left, she looked into my eyes.

"I'll be waiting."

I smiled and marked the date of the festival on my calendar. Dad came up to my room.

"Your friend just left with a big smile on her face. What did you do?"

"I just made a simple challenge for myself."

I picked up my pencil as my Dad looked at me proudly.

Emily and I continued to work for our clubs. Finally, the festival rolled around again. This time, I was able to see the incredible amount of work involved behind the scenes. Emily looked more and more exhausted with each passing day. She often kept going to sleep after the club dispersed. I would gently wake her up and make sure she got home safely. Two weeks to the festival. The anthology was progressing at a great speed. I decided to convey all my feelings for her through this cover. I worked hard on it day and night. One day, I was helping another club prepare its banner. It took a long time but we all managed to finish it before the school closed. One of the girls climbed the ladder to hang the banner outside the classroom. She leaned slightly and the ladder became unstable. She fell from the ladder. My body immediately moved. I caught her before she fell. The moment I caught her, I felt an intense pain in my right wrist. I gently set her down.

"Are you alright?"

The girl looked pale.

"I'm fine. Thank you so much."

I touched her shoulder lightly to assure her and steadied the ladder. I climbed up and hung it myself. Everyone thanked me and I walked away. My wrist was still hurting. I decided to go to the infirmary just in case. The school nurse looked at my hand and sighed.

"You've sprained it. I recommend you to just take rest and let it heal."

"I can't do that. I have work to do."

She placed her hand on my head.

"It's not a suggestion. If you don't want it to become worse, then let it rest."

She bandaged up my hand tightly. I thanked her and walked out of the infirmary. No. I can't rest now. I have to work on the cover. Yes, the cover. That's what's important now. I ripped off the bandage and threw it in the trash. Emily doesn't need to know about this. I entered the Art Club room and started working on the cover. The pain worsened with each minute. I couldn't draw straight. When Emily entered the room, I hid the cover from her.

"You want to keep it a surprise from me? I'm the Literature Club president."

"This isn't a simple cover for me."

"Ok, I understand. I'm done with my club. Are you coming?"

"I'll stay here and work for a while."

"See you tomorrow then."

"Bye, Emily."

As soon as she left, I breathed a sigh of relief. I continued working on the cover. The pain somehow kept me focused yet distracted. The final week of preparations, I was almost done with the cover. But when I looked at it, I couldn't find an ounce of love in it anymore. It all felt agonizing. The next day, as I opened the Art Club door, I saw Emily standing before my cover. She asked the other members to leave for a few minutes.

"What's up, Emily?"

She had tears in her eyes.

"Why didn't you tell me before?"

"Tell you what?"

She looked down at my hands.

"Why is your right hand shaking so much?"

"I might be getting a fever or something. I feel a little cold."

She came closer and grabbed my right hand. I winced in pain.

"Is this a fever?"

"How did you know?"

She pointed to the cover.

"What is this? It's very obvious that you're in pain. The art itself is screaming at me."

I looked closer and saw that I had made lots of blunders. Was I not able to notice it before because of the pain?

"Why did you hide it?"

A tear streamed down her face.

"You hid it from me all this while, didn't you? You kept painting even when you were in so much pain."

"Emily …"

"Why did you hide it?"

"Because this meant a lot to me. I didn't want to forsake it. There's only one cultural festival for us. I can't lose this chance!"

She came closer and placed her hand on my chest.

"What if you were unable to paint anymore? What if something happened to you? For me, that thought is scarier. Your health is more important to me than your art."

She walked out of the room. I stood there silently, not knowing what to do. I didn't see Emily again that day. After school ended, I walked to the hospital and got treated. My sprain became worse and I had to rest my right hand for an entire month. The next day, I apologized to everyone in the Art Club. They all forgave me and began finishing the anthology cover. Emily barely talked to me. This time, the cultural festival flashed by without any great memories. Coming to school felt drab. I constantly sulked at school and at home. Wanting a change of scenery, I grabbed a ladder and climbed the side of the house. I stood upon the roof. The strong breeze combined with the orange sky was just the scenery I needed. I felt like drawing this scenery. My injury would completely heal in a few days, so I didn't need to wait long for it. As I was enjoying the scenery, I heard a lot of noises. I looked towards the ladder and saw a figure trying to climb it. I quickly rushed towards Emily and grabbed her.

"What are you doing here?!"

"I saw you from below and I wanted to talk to you."

"You could've just waited for me to come down!"

"It didn't occur to me."

I quickly grabbed her as she almost slipped.

She hugged me tightly.

"I thought you were going to fall!"

She slowly comforted me. After making sure she was safe, I let go of her. The two of us stood next to each other and looked across the orange sky. Standing on top of this roof, even the biggest of my problems would be eclipsed by this beautiful scene.

"I always come here when I'm feeling troubled. The scenery you get to see from here always cheers me up." I squeezed Emily's hand.

"I'm sorry about hiding my injury from you."

"It's ok. I forgave you instantly. I missed you a lot. We didn't spend a lot of time together at the festival."

I sighed.

"It sucks that I wasn't able to draw for the culture festival. It would've made for the perfect confession."

She raised her eyebrows.

I quickly realized what I had said and looked away.

"I was looking forward to it as well."

She held up my injured hand.

"If you're in trouble, tell me. I'm here for you. Don't hide anything from me."

"I promise."

She linked her arms with mine.

"Since you missed your opportunity at the cultural festival, when will you try again? I don't have infinite patience."

I turned to the ladder.

"I'll do it now!"

Emily tugged on my arm.

"Wait, you're still injured!"

I pulled her into a hug.

"I'll draw for you for the rest of my life."

"I'll be looking forward to it."

We stayed on the roof for a while. The two of us held each other's hands tightly. That instant was the most precious moment for the both of us.

EIGHT YEARS LATER

I helped Prez put on his tuxedo.

"I can't believe you two are actually getting married. And she's pregnant! Prez, you're insane!"

Prez looked even paler.

"Don't mess with me. I wonder why I chose you as my best man. You're supposed to help me calm down."

I laughed and patted him on the shoulder.

"It'll be fine, Prez. I know how much you love her. Let's go now."

I walked with Prez and we stood in front of the altar. Leah came in dressed up in a beautiful wedding gown. Prez inhaled deeply and stood beside her. Emily stood next to me. During the wedding party, Leah and Prez walked up to us. Leah hugged the both of us tightly.

"It's been so long, how are you two!"

"So much has happened."

I smiled.

"You became a published author, Prez became Dad's apprentice."

Prez sighed.

"And your dad is insanely strict."

I laughed. Leah turned the questions on me.

"When is your marriage going to happen?"

I looked at Emily who was reading a thick book intently.

"Uh, it'll take a while for sure."

Emily pulled out a package and handed it to me.

"Oh, I forgot. Leah and Prez, this is for you!"

"What's this?"

Leah opened the wrapper and gasped in delight.

"Did you two make this?!"

"A special, original storybook. We wanted the two of you to be the first one to receive it."

On the book, Emily and my names were written in bold. The cover showed an orange sunset with two people standing on the roof. The cover design that was packed with years of love and emotion. It was the image of the happiest moment in two people's lives.

The moment of eternity frozen in souls who know how to love.

www.ingramcontent.com/pod-product-compliance
Lightning Source LLC
LaVergne TN
LVHW051452170726
843492LV00002B/650

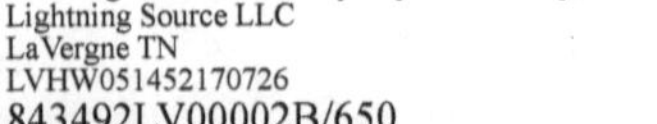